BY ROBERT MUCHAMORE

The Henderson's Boys series:

The CHERUB series:

Look out for CHERUB 12: Shadow Wave
Coming late 2010

A Catalogue record for this book is available
from the British Library

ISBN-13: 978 0 340 95648 9

Typeset in Goudy by Avon DataSet Ltd,
Bidford-on-Avon, Warwickshire

Printed and bound in Great Britain by
CPI Bookmarque Ltd, Croydon, Surrey

The paper and board used in this paperback by
Hodder Children's Books are natural recyclable products
made from wood grown in sustainable forests.
The manufacturing processes conform to the
environmental regulations of the country of origin.

Hodder Children's Books
A division of Hachette Children's Books
338 Euston Road, London NW1 3BH
An Hachette UK company
www.hachette.co.uk

THE ESCAPE
Robert Muchamore

Hodder
Children's
Books

A division of Hachette Children's Books

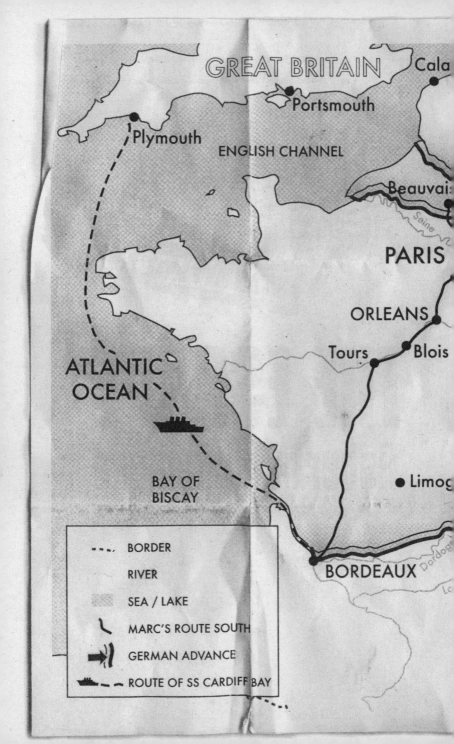

FRANCE 1940 – THE GERMAN ADVANCE

BRUSSELS

BELGIUM

GERMANY

German Front Line
JUNE 3RD 1940

LUX.

★ LUXEMBOURG

German Front Line
JUNE 12TH 1940

Rhine

● Strasbourg

Danube

FRANCE

● Dijon

AUS

★ BERN

SWITZERLAND

Loire

Rhône

● Lyon

● MILAN

ITALY

German Front Line
JUNE 25TH 1940

MEDITERRANEAN
SEA

● Marseille

Part One

5 June 1940 – 6 June 1940

Nazi Germany launched its invasion of France on 10 May 1940. On paper, the forces of France and her British allies were equal or superior to the Germans'. Most commentators predicted a long and bloody war. But whilst the allied armies spread out in defensive formations the Germans used the radical new tactic of blitzkrieg – massing tanks and armour into huge battle groups and punching through enemy lines.

By 21 May the Germans had successfully occupied a huge section of northern France. The British were forced into a humiliating sea evacuation at Dunkirk and the French army was in tatters. German generals wanted to push on towards Paris, but Hitler ordered them to pause, regroup and secure their supply lines.

On the night of June 3rd, he finally gave orders to resume the attack.

CHAPTER ONE

As a baby, Marc Kilgour had been abandoned between two stone flower pots on the platform at Beauvais station, sixty kilometres north of Paris. A porter found him lying inside a wooden fruit box and rushed him into the warmth of the stationmaster's office. There he discovered the only clue to the boy's identity – a scrap of notepaper with four handwritten words: *Allergic to cows' milk.*

Now twelve years old, Marc had imagined his abandonment so often that his memory of it seemed real: the frosty platform, his anxious mother kissing his cheek before boarding a train and disappearing for ever, her eyes moist and her head crammed with secrets as the carriages steamed into the night. In his fantasies Marc saw a statue being erected on the platform some day. Marc Kilgour: fighter ace, Le Mans race winner, hero of France . . .

But his life so far could hardly have been less exciting. He'd grown up in a decrepit farmhouse a few kilometres north of Beauvais, its cracked walls and shrivelled beams constantly threatened by the destructive power of a hundred orphan boys.

The region's farms, chateaux and forests were attractive to Parisians who came out for a Sunday drive; but it was hell to Marc, and the windows into more exciting lives he got through the radio and magazines tormented him.

His days were all the same: the squirming mass of orphans rising to the crack of a walking stick on a metal radiator, school until lunchtime, then an afternoon toiling on a nearby farm. It was brutal work, but the men who were supposed to do it had been called up to fight the Germans.

Morel's farm was the largest in the area and Marc was the youngest of four boys who worked there. Mr Tomas, the orphanage director, took advantage of the shortage of labour and received a good price for the boys' work; but the lads saw none of the money and any suggestion that they should was met with a stern expression and a lecture on how much each of them had already cost in food and clothing.

A long history of run-ins with Director Tomas had earned Marc the least pleasant job on the farm. Most of Morel's land produced wheat and vegetables, but the farmer kept a dozen dairy cows in a shed whilst their calves were raised for veal under an adjacent canopy. Morel had no land for pasture, so his cattle lived on fodder and only glimpsed daylight when they were led to a neighbouring farm for a romp with Henri the bull.

While his fellow orphans tended fields, Marc clambered amidst the tightly packed stalls, scrubbing out the milking shed. An adult cow produces a hundred and twenty litres of faeces and urine each day and takes no account of holidays or weekends.

Seven days a week, Marc found himself in the vile-smelling shed, scraping manure down a sloped floor into the slurry pit. When the trampled straw and muck was cleared, he had to hose the concrete and replenish each stall with bales of hay and vegetable waste. Twice a week came the worst job of all: shovelling out the slurry pit and wheeling the stinking barrels to a barn, where they would rot down before being used as fertiliser.

*

Jae Morel was also twelve and had known Marc since their first day at school. Marc was a handsome boy, with tangled blond hair, and Jae had always liked him. But as the daughter of the area's wealthiest farmer she wasn't expected to mix with boys who came to school with bare feet. At age nine she'd moved from the village school to an all girls' academy in Beauvais and had almost forgotten Marc; until he'd begun working on her father's farm a few months earlier.

At first the pair only nodded and smiled, but since the weather had turned fine they'd managed a few conversations while sitting together in the grass, and occasionally Jae would share a bar of chocolate. They both sought a deeper connection, but their talk centred on local gossip and reminiscences from the days when they'd shared a classroom.

Jae always approached the cow shed as if she was taking a stroll and couldn't care less, but she often doubled back or hid in the long grass before standing up and pretending to bump into Marc by accident as he came outside. The process was strangely exciting, even though they'd never exchanged more than words and chocolate.

On this particular Wednesday, Jae was surprised to see Marc emerge from the side door of the cow shed, bare-chested and in a vile temper. He lashed out with his rubber boot, sending a metal bucket clattering across the farmyard before he grabbed another and put it under the tap mounted on the shed's exterior.

Intrigued by Marc's fury, Jae hunkered down and leaned against the trunk of an elm. She watched as Marc wriggled out of his filthy boots then glanced around furtively before removing his under-shorts, trousers and the socks into which they were tucked. Jae had never seen a boy naked and clapped a hand over her mouth as Marc stepped up on to a large paving slab and grabbed a block of soap.

Marc cupped his hands and dipped them into the bucket, splashing water on himself before working the soap. The water was cold and even though the sun was hot he moved hurriedly. When he was lathered all over, he raised the bucket high into the air and drained the water over his head.

Soap burned his eyes as he reached out for a grotty towel wrapped over a wooden post.

'You've got a big arse!' Jae shouted, as she sprang out of the grass.

Marc urgently flicked the damp hair off his face and was stunned to see Jae's brown eyes and sweet smile. He dropped the towel and lunged towards a pair of corduroy trousers.

'Jesus,' he choked, as the usually simple task of stepping into trousers became a frantic bout of hopping. 'How long have you been there?'

'Long enough.' Jae grinned, pointing at a wooden

screen lying flat on the pathway.

'I don't usually bother pulling it up . . . You're never around until later.'

'No school,' Jae explained. 'Some of the teachers have left. The Boche[1] are on the march . . .'

Marc nodded as he buttoned his trousers and lobbed his work boots into the shed. 'Did you hear the artillery shells earlier?'

'Made me jump,' Jae replied. 'And the German planes! One of our maids said there were fires in town, near the marketplace.'

'You can smell burning when the wind changes . . . Your dad's got that swanky Renault. You should head south.'

Jae shook her head. 'My mother wants to leave, but Daddy reckons the Germans won't bother us if we don't bother them. He says they'll still need farmers, whether it's French or German crooks running the country.'

'The director let us listen to the radio for a while last night,' Marc said. 'They said we're planning a counterattack. We could drive the Boche out.'

'Maybe,' Jae said uncertainly. 'But it doesn't look good . . .'

Marc didn't need Jae to explain further. The

---

[1] Boche – offensive term for German people.

government radio stations bristled with optimistic talk about fighting back and broadcast stirring speeches on *turning points* and the *French fighting spirit*. But no amount of propaganda could disguise truckloads of injured troops retreating from the front.

'It's too depressing,' Marc said, buttoning his shirt as he smiled at Jae. 'I wish I was old enough to fight. Have you heard anything from your brothers?'

'Nothing . . . But nobody knows about anyone. The post has gone to hell. They're probably being held prisoner. Or they might have escaped at Dunkirk.'

Marc nodded optimistically. 'BBC France said over a hundred thousand of our troops made it across the channel with the Brits.'

'So why were you in such a mood?' Jae asked.

'When?'

'Just now,' she smirked. 'When you steamed out of the shed and kicked the bucket.'

'Oh, *that*. I was all set to finish when I realised I'd left my shovel in one of the pens. So I reached in to grab it, the cow's tail shoots up and VOOM. It shits right in my face – mouth was open too . . .'

'EWW!' Jae shrieked, stepping back in horror. 'I don't know how you work in there! Just the smell makes me gag, and if *that* went in my mouth I'd die.'

'Get used to anything, I guess. And your dad's all right

in some ways. He knows it's a filthy job, so I only have to work half as long as the boys in the fields and he gave me boots and some of your brothers' old clothes. They're too big, but at least I don't have to go around stinking of slurry.'

After the initial shock Jae saw the funny side and she re-enacted the scene, flicking her arm up like the cow's tail and making a noise. 'VOOM – SPLAT!'

Marc was irked. 'It's not funny. I've still got the taste in my mouth.'

But this only made Jae laugh harder and Marc got annoyed.

'Little rich girl,' he sniped. '*You* wouldn't like it. You'd be crying your eyes out.'

'VOOM – SPLAT!' Jae repeated. She'd made herself laugh so hard that her legs were buckling.

'I'll show you what it's like,' Marc said, lunging forwards and wrapping his arms around her back.

'*No,*' Jae protested, kicking out as he hitched her off the ground. She was impressed by his strength, but she pounded bony fists against his back as he marched towards the open slurry pit at the end of the barn.

'I'll tell my dad!' she squealed. 'You'll be in so much trouble.'

'VOOM – SPLAT!' Marc replied, as he swung Jae forwards so that her long hair dangled precariously over the foul-smelling pit. The stench had the physical presence of a slap. 'Do you fancy a swim?'

'Put me down,' Jae demanded, her stomach churning as she looked at the flies on the bubbling crust of manure. 'You oaf. If I get one speck of that on me you'll be *so* dead.'

Jae was starting to wriggle and Marc realised he didn't have the strength to hold her for much longer, so he swung her around and planted her back on the ground.

'Idiot,' she hissed, holding her stomach and retching.

'But it seemed so funny when it happened to *me*,' Marc said.

'Pig head,' Jae growled, as she swept her hair back into place.

'Maybe the princess should go back to her big house and practise her Mozart,' Marc teased, before making a screeching noise like a badly played violin.

Jae was spitting mad, not so much because of what Marc had just done, but because she'd let herself get so fond of him.

'Mother always told me to stay away from your type,' Jae said, squinting fiercely into the sunlight at him. 'Orphans! Look at you, you've just washed but even your clean clothes are filthy rags.'

'Temper, temper,' Marc grinned.

'Marc Kilgour, no wonder you work with manure. You *are* manure.'

Marc was anxious that Jae calm down. She was making a tonne of noise, and Farmer Morel prized his only daughter.

'Take it easy,' Marc begged. 'Us lads muck around, you know? I'm sorry. I'm not used to girls.'

Jae charged forwards and tried to slap Marc across the face, but he dodged out of the way. She swung around to catch him across the back of the head, but her canvas plimsoll skidded on the dry earth and she found herself doing the splits.

Marc reached around to save Jae as her front foot slid forwards, but her smock slipped through his fingers and he could only watch as she toppled into the pit.

CHAPTER TWO

The first bombs fell on Paris on the night of 3 June. It was the first sign of the German advance and the explosions were the starting pistol for an evacuation of the city.

The Nazi regime had terrorised Warsaw following the invasion of Poland the year before and Parisians were expecting the same treatment: Jews and government officials shot in the streets, girls raped, homes looted and all men of fighting age taken to labour camps. While many Parisians fled – by train, car or even on foot – others carried on with their lives and were widely regarded as fools by those who were leaving.

Paul Clarke was a slightly-built eleven year old and one of the dwindling number of pupils who still attended

Paris' largest English-language school. The school served British children whose parents worked in the city but weren't rich enough to send their offspring to a boarding school back home. They were the children of embassy clerks, low-ranking military attachés, drivers and others of similar status in private companies.

Since the beginning of May the pupil roll had fallen from three hundred to less than fifty. Most teachers had also gone south or returned to Britain, and the remaining kids – who ranged from five up to sixteen – were now taught a shambolic curriculum in the school's wood-panelled main hall, overlooked by King George and a map of the British Empire.

By 3 June the only teacher left was the school's founder and headmistress, Mrs Divine. Her typist had been drafted in as a classroom assistant.

Paul was a daydreamer and he much preferred this emergency arrangement to the years he'd spent seated rigidly amongst boys his own age, getting rapped on the knuckles with a wooden ruler whenever his mind wandered.

The work set by the elderly headmistress wasn't up to Paul's intelligence and this left him with time to doodle. There was hardly an exercise book or scrap of paper in Paul's desk that wasn't covered with delicately inked drawings. His preference was for armoured knights and fire-breathing dragons, but he could also make accurate drawings of sports cars and aeroplanes.

Presently, Paul's ink-blotched fingers were pencilling the outline of a French biplane diving heroically towards a line of German tanks. The drawing had been requested by one of the younger boys, at the price of one Toblerone bar.

'Hey, skinny,' a girl said, as she flicked Paul's ear and made him smudge the tip of a propeller.

'For god's sake,' he said furiously, as he looked around and scowled at his older sister.

Rosie Clarke was thirteen and as different from Paul as siblings can be. There was some likeness in the eyes and they shared dark hair and a freckled complexion, but where Paul's clothes drooped as if they were ashamed to hang from his thin body, Rosie had a buffalo's shoulders, a precocious set of breasts and long nails that regularly drew her younger brother's blood.

'Rosemarie Clarke,' Mrs Divine said, in a posh English accent. 'How many times must I tell you to leave your brother alone?'

Paul appreciated having the teacher onside, but her remark also reminded the entire class that he got bullied by his sister and the mirth that rippled across the room was all at his expense.

'Madame, our father's outside,' Rosie explained.

Paul snapped his head towards the window. He'd been engrossed in drawing and hadn't seen the dark blue Citroën roll into the school courtyard. A glance at the clock over the blackboard confirmed that it was a good hour before home time.

'Mrs Divine!' Mr Clarke swooned, as he entered the hall a moment later. 'I'm *so* sorry to disturb your lesson.'

The headmistress showed obvious distaste as Paul and Rosie's dad kissed her on both cheeks. Clarke was the French sales representative for the Imperial Wireless Company. He dressed flamboyantly, in a dark suit, mirror-finished shoes and a polka-dot cravat that Mrs Divine found vulgar; but her expression warmed when Mr Clarke handed her a cheque.

'We've got to collect some things from our apartment and then we're heading south,' he explained. 'I've paid up until the end of term – I want the school to be here when things get back to normal.'

'That's most kind,' Mrs Divine said. She'd spent thirty years building the school from nothing and seemed genuinely touched as she produced a handkerchief from the sleeve of her cardigan and dabbed her eye.

It was Paul and Rosie's turn to play out the goodbye scene they'd seen many times over the past month. Boys shook hands like gentlemen, while departing girls tended to cry, hug and promise to write letters.

Paul found the stiff upper lip easy, because he'd never been popular and his favourite art teacher and two closest friends had already gone. Feeling rather awkward, he stepped towards the younger boys at the front of the room and returned the exercise book to its eight-year-old owner.

'Guess I won't get it done now,' he said apologetically. 'It's outlined in pencil, so you could finish it yourself.'

'You're *so* good,' the boy said, admiring the explosion around a half drawn tank as he opened his desk. 'I'll leave it. I'd only ruin it.'

Paul was going to refuse payment until he saw that the boy's desk contained more than a dozen triangular bars. Toblerone in hand, Paul stepped back to his desk and gathered his belongings into a leather satchel: pens and ink, a stack of battered comic books and the two artist's pads with all of his best drawings in them. Meanwhile Rosie had erupted like a volcano.

'We'll all be back some day,' she bawled theatrically, as she crushed the wind out of her best friend, Grace.

Upon seeing this, two of Rosie's other friends backed away.

'Don't worry, Dad,' Paul said, as he approached the doorway and saw the bewilderment on his father's face. 'It's just girls; they're all a bit nuts.'

Paul realised that Mrs Divine was holding out her

hand and he shook it. She was a cold fish and he'd never really liked her, but he'd been a pupil for five years and the gnarled fingers seemed sad.

'Thank you for everything,' he said. 'I hope the Germans don't do anything horrible when they get here.'

'Paul,' Mr Clarke snapped, gently cuffing his son around the head. 'Don't say things like *that*.'

By this time Rosie had finished crushing her friends and tears streaked as she shook both Mrs Divine and her typist by the hand. Paul waved to nobody in particular as he followed his father down the school's main corridor and outside on to a short flight of steps.

The sun shone brightly on the paved courtyard as Paul headed towards the rather impressive Citroën. The sky was cloudless, but the school was on a hill overlooking the city and smoke poured from several buildings in the centre.

'I didn't hear any bombs,' Rosie noted, joining them.

'The government's moving south,' Mr Clarke explained. 'They're burning everything they can't carry. The defence ministry has even set some of its own buildings on fire.'

'Why are they leaving?' Paul asked. 'I thought there was supposed to be a counterattack?'

'Don't be naive, you baby,' Rosie sneered.

'We might not be in this mess if our side had decent

radios,' Mr Clarke said bitterly. 'The German forces are communicating instantly. The French use messengers on horseback. I tried to sell a radio system to the French army, but their generals are living in the dark ages.'

Paul was shocked to see a cascade of papers come at him as he opened the back door of his father's car.

'Don't let the wind get them!' Mr Clarke gasped, as he dived forwards and scooped manila folders off the pavement.

Paul shut the door before anything else escaped, then peered through the glass and saw that the entire back seat was covered in folders and loose papers.

'Imperial Wireless Company records,' Mr Clarke explained. 'I had to leave the office in a hurry.'

'Why?' Rosie asked.

But her father ignored the question and opened the front passenger door. 'Paul, I think it's best if you clamber in between the front seats. I want you to stack those papers as we drive. Rosie, you get in the front.'

Paul thought his father sounded tense. 'Is everything OK, Dad?'

'Of course.' Mr Clarke nodded, giving Paul his best salesman's smile as the boy squeezed between the front seats. 'I've just had a hell of a morning. I tried four garages to get petrol and ended up having to beg at the British Embassy.'

'The Embassy?' Rosie said curiously, as she slammed the passenger door.

'They've got a reserve supply for getting staff out in an emergency,' Mr Clarke explained. 'Luckily I know a few faces there, but it cost me a bob or two.'

Mr Clarke wasn't rich, but his six-cylinder Citroën was a grand affair that belonged to the Imperial Wireless Company. Paul always enjoyed being in the luxurious rear compartment, with its crushed velvet seats, mahogany trim and tasselled blinds over the windows.

'Do these papers go in any order?' he asked, clearing a space for his bum as his father drove out of the courtyard.

'Just stack them up,' Mr Clarke said, as Rosie looked back and waved at her friend Grace, who was standing on the courtyard steps. 'I'll get a suitcase from the apartment.'

'So where are we going?' Paul asked.

'I'm not sure,' Mr Clarke said. 'South, obviously. The last I heard there were still passenger ferries heading to Britain from Bordeaux. If not, we should be able to cross into Spain and get a boat from Bilbao.'

'And if we can't cross into Spain?' Rosie asked nervously, as Paul straightened an armful of papers by tapping them against the leather armrest.

'Well . . .' Mr Clarke said uncertainly. 'We won't know for sure until we get down south, but don't worry. Britain has the biggest merchant fleet and the most powerful navy in the world. There'll be a boat heading somewhere.'

By this time the Citroën was cruising briskly downhill, past rows of apartment blocks with the occasional shop or café at ground level. Around half of the businesses were closed or boarded up, while others continued to trade despite frequent signs indicating shortages, such as *no butter* on food stores, or *tobacco only available with a meal* on the outside of cafés.

'Shouldn't we stop at the florist?' Rosie asked.

Mr Clarke glanced solemnly at his daughter. 'I know I promised, sweetheart, but the cemetery's fifteen kilometres in the wrong direction. We need to pack quickly and get as far out of Paris as we can.'

'But,' Rosie said sadly, 'what if we can't come back? We might never see Mum's grave again.'

This thought made Paul freeze as he stacked the last of the papers. The cemetery always made Paul cry. Then his dad would cry and stand around the grave for ages, even when it was freezing cold. It was always horrible and he rather liked the idea of never going back.

'Rosie, we're not leaving your mother behind,' Mr Clarke said. 'She'll be up there watching over us the whole way.'

CHAPTER THREE

Marc sat in the orphanage kitchen wearing nothing but a pair of grubby shorts. Director Tomas had ordered him to keep absolutely still, with his head down and his palms flat against the long wooden table. His stomach rumbled as two young nuns baked bread in the wood-fired ovens, whilst a huge bowl of vegetable soup bubbled on the stove.

Marc knew he wouldn't be allowed supper and smiled edgily when Sister Madeline placed a small plate with cheese, sausage and chopped vegetables in front of him.

'Eat quickly,' the nun whispered, aiming a glance towards the door. 'The director will reprimand me if he catches us.'

Marc was grateful for the food and scoffed it down without chewing, then shoved the plate across the table.

While the young nun was willing to help, Marc's fellow orphans had less sympathy. Boys halted in the kitchen doorway and poked out tongues, wagged fingers and whispered nastily about the beating he was going to get and how he wouldn't be able to sit down for a week. Outside, in plain view of the kitchen window, younger boys enacted a pantomime of mock beatings, a hanging and even a firing squad until the older nun rapped on the glass and told them to leave Marc alone.

Marc didn't really mind. Orphanage life was all he'd known and bullying seemed as natural as breathing. Teasing a kid who faced a beating and trying to make him cry was just one of many rituals the orphans had devised to torture each other. As one of the stronger lads, Marc had inflicted his share of suffering on the weaker kids, and had learned never to give an inch when older boys or the staff started on him.

But he *was* scared of the director. Jae Morel ending up in a slurry pit was a serious matter and the fact that it wasn't entirely his fault counted for nothing. Director Tomas was going to give him the beating of his life; the kind he usually reserved for boys who stole from the village shop or ran away.

While fear pricked Marc's every thought it was falling out with Jae that hurt deep down. Their relationship had amounted to little, but her friendship had made Marc feel like something more than a shit-shovelling orphan for the first time in his life.

Unfortunately, Jae had called him much worse than that when she'd emerged from the pit, encrusted in manure. Farmer Morel had sacked him on the spot and threatened to remove certain sensitive elements of his anatomy with a blunt knife if he ever came near his daughter or his farm again.

The door of the office across the hallway opened and the heavily built director emerged, clutching the neck of a sobbing seven year old called Jean. A shove sent the youngster sprawling across the tiled kitchen floor, and the squat man looked pleased with himself as he ran a hand across his glistening bald scalp.

Sister Madeline looked horrified at the red welts on the boy's skinny back.

'Put some iodine on his cuts, sister,' the director ordered, as Jean grabbed the table to pull himself up. 'And if you wet the bed again, you'll be sleeping out in the barn with the chickens.'

'Yes, sir. Sorry, sir,' the boy sniffed, rubbing his tiny hands together.

Director Tomas raised one eyebrow and clapped as he turned towards Marc. 'And after the warm-up, we have the main event,' he said, gleefully pointing an arm towards the office.

Marc was a regular on the director's beating schedule and he always imagined heroics at this stage: pulling a dagger out of his pocket, or grabbing the saucepan and throwing boiling soup in the director's face. But as always, he didn't have the guts, so he stepped solemnly towards the office, with its leather-topped desk and the smell of cigarettes mixed with BO.

Tomas was a powerful man who'd boxed middleweight during his army days. Middle age had fattened him up, but though a few fifteen and sixteen year olds had swung at him over the years, none had ever come off better for it.

'Stand straight. Feet apart, hands out front,' the director barked, as he slammed his office door.

Across the hall, Jean cried noisily as the nun used iodine to disinfect his cuts. Another pleasure Marc had to look forward to.

'Hasn't been long since you were last here, Kilgour,' Director Tomas said. 'But now you've *really* excelled yourself.'

The director swiped his long cane from an umbrella stand and ran a piece of rag along its length to wipe away Jean's blood. The cane had a metal tip to cause extra pain and the director whooshed it through the air before jamming the end into Marc's nose, stretching his nostril and forcing him to snap his chin up towards the gloomy ceiling.

'Morel is one of our most respected neighbours,' Tomas growled. 'What was going on between you and his daughter?'

'Nothing,' Marc said, as the metal tip burrowed deeper into his nose.

'And how does *nothing* lead to the poor girl emerging from a pit encrusted in manure?'

'We just spoke a few times. We had a little bit of an argument and she fell into the pit by accident. I tried to save her.'

The director pulled the cane out of Marc's nose and lashed it across his face. The blow was a shock and Marc stumbled back to the door, clutching his cheek. He'd known it was going to be bad, but he'd never heard of the director striking a boy across the face before.

'Stand up straight,' the director ordered. 'Get that hand off your cheek before I knock it off.'

'Yes, sir.'

'How many times do I have to hit you, Kilgour?' the director snarled, as a second blow slammed into Marc's naked side, just below his ribcage. 'I've seen boys like you. Nasty, scheming boys, whose lives always end at a shot in the head or a penal colony.'[2]

---

[2] Penal colony – a prison in the French colonies where inmates were expected to do backbreaking physical work.

After a third stroke, the director bundled Marc against the desk and pressed his chest to the cracked leather top.

'Haven't you got anything to say for yourself, boy?'

Marc was scared of the pain, but the director had beaten him regularly since he was five years old. He'd never shown weakness and had no intention of giving the director any satisfaction now.

'I guess it's a shame I lost the job,' Marc said. 'You've had a new bicycle and two new suits since the four of us started working for Morel.'

He expected the remark to trigger a savage caning, but it was going to happen anyway and he wanted it over with. However, instead of using the cane, the director brought his knee up between Marc's legs with such force that his feet lifted off the floor.

Marc groaned as he rolled over the side of the desk and crashed to the floor. He'd snagged a cord and a telephone crashed down on top of him, followed by the director's heel, pressing on his stomach.

'See where a smart mouth gets you?' the director gloated, bending his cane as he loomed over the boy. 'You're nothing, understand? A dog would offer companionship, a pig is good for meat and a chicken lays eggs, but an orphan boy is worth nothing.'

The pain in Marc's balls was so bad that he fought for

breath. The director took his shoe off and began lashing out with the cane.

'This doesn't hurt me one bit,' the director beamed, as the beating continued.

By this time Marc had rolled himself in a ball. His naked torso was covered in red lines and pain came from twenty different places.

'Do you think you're tough?' the director said, as he stopped the thrashing to catch his breath. 'I don't think I've *ever* seen you cry.'

Marc took his hands away from his face and tried to look defiant, but he was losing his battle with a trembling bottom lip.

'I've almost broken you this time, haven't I, Kilgour?' the director grinned. 'Give me another few minutes and I'll have you sobbing as hard as little Jean.'

The office door swung inwards and Sister Madeline hurried into the room with a tray of bread and soup.

'Haven't you heard of knocking, woman?' Tomas bellowed.

But the young nun set the wooden tray on the desktop with a defiant clatter. 'Sausage and vegetable soup,' she said, as she moved towards Marc and reached out her hand.

The director was furious. 'What are you doing, girl? Get *out*.'

The young nun pretended not to hear. 'I'll clean his wounds now that you're finished.'

The director gave Sister Madeline a look that seemed to question her sanity. 'And what makes you so sure that I've finished with him? I might have barely begun.'

'Marc has had *enough*, Director,' she said, trying to sound firm, but clearly frightened. 'Enough.'

Marc rolled on to his bum and sat up, but the director stepped in front of him.

'This is my office and my orphanage,' he boomed. 'I deal with the boys as I see fit and if you don't get back to the kitchen this instant I'll report you to the bishop.'

The young nun clenched her fists. 'Very well,' she said. 'And when I'm brought before the bishop, I'll be sure to mention your new suits and the bicycle. I'm *sure* you'll be able to make a proper account of all the money paid by Mr Morel.'

The director reddened as he reared up on his heels and hurtled his cane back into the umbrella stand. 'Take the boy then,' he growled.

'Thank you, Director,' the sister said, nodding obligingly as she helped Marc on to his bare feet. 'I hope you enjoy the soup, sir.'

Marc bunched his fists and bit down on his lip, determined not to let the pain show. He knew he owed Sister Madeline, but he was too upset to speak as she led him down the hallway and into a small room with a bed and a sink that was used as a sickbay.

There were boys playing outside and the sister shut the door and pulled the curtain before they got a chance to gloat about the state he was in. Marc sat on the edge of a small bed – ironically, his bum was one of the few parts of his body that wasn't injured – while Sister Madeline ran a face cloth under the cold tap. She smiled reassuringly as she sat down and began dabbing the blood from his cheek.

'Thank you for . . .' Marc said, but he stopped before he broke down.

'You don't have to be proud,' Sister Madeline said, as streaks of pink water drizzled down Marc's face. 'We're all humble before God.'

'I didn't mean to do anything to Jae,' Marc said, stifling a sob. 'She was . . . We had a laugh together. Now I'll never see her again . . .'

Marc rested his head against the nun's floury apron as he began to cry openly. She wanted to put an arm around his back, but he had cuts all over and she didn't want to hurt him even more.

CHAPTER FOUR

Mrs Mujard stood on the front steps of a five-storey apartment block, trying to get her money's worth out of a cigarette stub. The elderly woman had been the building's concierge for more than thirty years and could now barely move on the lattice of varicose veins that passed for her legs.

Her eyebrows shot up guiltily when she saw Mr Clarke's Citroën swing into a parking bay across the street and she shuffled back to the chest-high reception desk as Rosie and Paul came into the lobby.

'Hello, Madame,' Paul said brightly. 'Any post?'

Mrs Mujard pulled three envelopes from one of the cubby holes behind her. Paul aimed his Toblerone at her.

'Chocolate?' he asked brightly.

The elderly lady shuddered. 'Sticks in my teeth.' And then she looked up at Mr Clarke, who'd stepped into the lobby holding his briefcase. 'I have news,' she said gloomily.

Mujard always had news. News could be anything from a new tenant to someone overfilling their bath and damaging the flat below. Recently, all of Mujard's news had been about tenants packing up to leave the city.

'I'd love to catch up on the gossip,' Mr Clarke said, 'but we're heading south. I want to get on the road as soon as possible.'

'The news is about *your* apartment, sir.'

Mujard never came straight out with a story. People were more inclined to stay and gossip if you fed them slivers.

'My apartment?' Mr Clarke asked, as Paul and Rosie turned away from the foot of the staircase.

'Yes sir,' Mujard said, nodding grimly, but making no attempt to go further.

Mr Clarke sounded impatient. 'What *about* our apartment?'

'The police.'

This hook was enough to make Paul and Rosie walk back to the reception desk.

'What would the police want with us?' Rosie asked.

Mujard shrugged and Mr Clarke slammed his palm on the countertop, making her jump. Paul and Rosie were startled. Their father was a mild man, but he definitely wasn't himself today.

'I have two children,' Mr Clarke said, almost begging. 'I need to get them out of the city. Now if you have information, *please* tell me quickly.'

Mujard looked offended. 'There's no need to shout,' she said, but she was secretly delighted by the outburst. 'Three detectives, plain clothes. They asked where you were and came with a warrant to search your apartment.'

Mr Clarke glanced at his watch. 'How long ago?'

'Two or three hours. They asked where you might be. I explained that you were a salesman and said you'd either be at your office, or on the road.'

Mr Clarke glanced anxiously at his car outside, then at the children. 'We need to leave Paris *now*.'

He grabbed Paul's arm and dragged him towards the street. 'What's going on?' the boy asked anxiously. 'Why are the police looking for you?'

'I don't think they are,' Mr Clarke said cryptically. 'I'll explain everything in the car.'

Rosie protested. 'But we're here now. I don't have a change of clothes, or a toothbrush or . . .'

Clarke thought for a second. It *was* a long journey and comforts such as a change of clothes and a few personal items would make it far more tolerable.

'I suppose,' he said, looking at Rosie. Then he

thanked Mujard for the information and began bounding up the narrow staircase to the fourth floor, taking the steps two at a time. 'We've got to be out of here in five minutes,' he continued. 'Grab some essentials: clothes, toiletries, small personal items. I don't want the car stuffed with toys and junk.'

The trio were breathless by the time they reached the door of apartment sixteen. Mujard had unlocked for the police officers, so the door was intact, but the apartment had been ransacked. Drawers were emptied over the floor, a tall lamp had been knocked down and one of the sofas had been tipped on its back with its bottom sliced open to see if anything was hidden inside.

Paul looked shaken as Rosie bent down and began gathering pieces of a broken Wedgwood plate that had belonged to her great-grandmother.

'Forget that,' Mr Clarke barked, grabbing his daughter's arm and hoisting her up. 'They're not police . . . I've told you I'll explain later. Right now we've got to pack up and leave.'

Mr Clarke gave Rosie a nudge towards her bedroom, then he walked into the kitchen and began opening cupboards, searching for food to take on the journey. Paul started towards his room, but he knew he'd need to pee before setting off so he cut into the bathroom and bolted the door.

Paul still missed his mother and the bathroom evoked her memory. He could remember splashing around in the bath with Rosie when they were little and his fascination with his mother's paraphernalia of perfumes, make-up and a giant glass jar stuffed with balls of cotton wool. Her half of the bathroom shelf was now clinically empty and he tried putting this out of mind as he unbuttoned his grey shorts and tried to pee.

'Thinking about it, you'd both better change clothes,' Mr Clarke shouted, from the living room. 'Your uniforms are very English. It's best if you blend in.'

Paul hurriedly washed his hands and was pulling his shirt over his head as he stepped out of the bathroom and clattered into Rosie. She was carrying a suitcase of clothes towards the front door.

'Watch it, bone head,' she yelled, shoving Paul against the wall.

Stupidly, Paul hadn't bothered undoing any of his shirt buttons and one of them popped off as he staggered blindly into his bedroom. He threw the shirt and the vest inside it on the bed and glanced around quickly, wondering which of his things he wanted to take. He decided on the alarm clock he'd had for Christmas, all of his clothes – he only had two pairs of long trousers and three shirts anyway – and as much of his painting and drawing equipment as he thought he'd be able to get away with without making his dad mad.

But before he could pack anything, Paul realised he'd need one of the cases stashed under the bed in his father's room. He spun around quickly, but was surprised to hear his bedroom door click shut and see a man step out from behind it.

Paul dropped his jaw to scream, but within a second a hand was clamped to his face. A fingertip slipped into his mouth and he bit down hard. The man hissed with pain, but it wasn't enough to stop him shoving Paul backwards on to the bed and pressing the barrel of a pistol against the bridge of his nose.

'Be silent, or die,' the man said.

His French sounded fluent, but his accent was unmistakeably German.

CHAPTER FIVE

Marc shared an attic bedroom with twenty other orphans. Their metal bunks were crammed so tight that boys who slept at the far end had to clamber over mattresses to get in or out. To make matters worse Director Tomas had ordered the only window nailed shut after a boy had tumbled out during a mass brawl, and the lack of fresh air left the room with a fragrance you'd be unlikely to find in any Paris boutique.

After Sister Madeline had patched him up, Marc had wiped his eyes and limped up four flights. He'd bloodied several noses to earn the privilege of a top bunk, but Marc's balls and stomach were agony as he struggled to haul himself on to the mattress. Despite the heat, pain and a couple of little kids jumping between the lower bunks and making a racket, Marc was exhausted and quickly fell asleep.

No boy caned by the director was allowed to eat until the following morning and, having slept through the early evening, Marc woke at nine p.m. and was annoyed to find himself wide awake, headachey and starving, as his roommates noisily stripped for bed.

Most boys had been playing outdoors and it was too hot for pyjamas, so the room thronged with sweaty limbs clambering over mattresses and shrill voices disputing the score of a football match. Some of the tiniest boys had trained themselves to ignore the noise and were already asleep.

Two stinking feet rested on the edge of Marc's mattress, centimetres from his face. He tried to sit up, intending to slap them away, but he moaned with pain as the congealed blood on his back ripped away from his sheets.

'Look who's awake,' the owner of the feet sneered, and before Marc knew it bodies were clambering over squeaking bed frames towards him. Nine-year-old Jacques, who slept below, stood on the edge of his bunk and peered over Marc's pillow. He got the first proper glance at his back.

'Holy *shit* that's bad,' Jacques gasped.

Six others were soon either trying to get behind Marc

or shouting requests for him to turn around so they could see his injuries.

'Does that hurt?' Jacques teased, as he pushed a finger against one of Marc's cuts.

'Piss off,' Marc shouted. 'Do that again and you'll get a punch.' But Marc was fond of his little bunkmate and Jacques knew it was an idle threat.

By this time someone had grabbed the heavily-stained blanket covering Marc's legs, revealing his most dramatic injury: a deep gash where the cane's metal tip had torn into his thigh.

'Nasty,' someone said as all the others backed away.

'And Tomas' heel mark on his belly,' another noted. 'He messed you up, Marc! What did you do?'

'Leave off,' Marc said grumpily, snatching his blanket back. But there were six lads in his face and he knew there was no way they'd give him any peace until he'd explained.

'Is it true you were snogging Jae Morel?' someone asked.

Marc's head was pounding, but the pressure was on. If he looked weak the lads would rip him to shreds.

'Sure,' Marc said, putting on a grin. 'She was all over me. I had my hands on her tits and everything.'

'You dog!' an older boy at the back of the crowd shouted.

But Marc's nemesis, Lanier, was determined to prick his bubble. All boys had their slot in the pecking order and behaved accordingly. The trouble was, Marc and Lanier fitted the same one. They were the same age, had the same kind of stocky physique, and the result was an intense rivalry that stretched all the way back to fighting over toys as toddlers.

'Jae Morel hasn't even got boobs,' Lanier snorted.

'How would you know?' Marc sneered. 'When did you last see her?'

'I spoke to Denis when he got back from Morel's fields,' Lanier said. 'He told me you went psycho and threw Jae in the slurry pit.'

Lanier's attempt to put Marc down for lying about getting off with a girl would have worked with teenagers, but Marc's audience was younger and in their eyes throwing a girl into a slurry pit was way better than kissing her.

'Totally worth the beating,' Jacques said loyally. 'Welts heal, legends live for ever!'

The rest of the crowd murmured in agreement and Lanier was furious. 'Well, you wait, Marc,' he said, wagging his finger. 'The director will find you a new job now and it'll be so much worse.'

Jacques shot Lanier a look of contempt. 'How could it be worse than mucking out cows?'

'I don't know,' Lanier said defensively, as his face reddened with anger. But he knew he was losing the argument so he dropped through the narrow gap between two mattresses and retreated between the tightly packed beds to his own on the far side of the room.

Meanwhile a scrawny fourteen year old called Gerard had stepped in and stood near the door unlacing his muddy work boots. He was the oldest boy who still slept on a lower bunk. He was jealous of Marc, but too weak to challenge him physically.

'You'll never *believe* what I saw,' Gerard told the room, with an air of sarcasm. 'The director had me repairing the front fence where that army truck clipped it. I came back in to put the tools away. You know that little cupboard under the stairs, opposite the sick room?'

There were a few nods and yeses as Marc realised what was coming.

'I could hear *little* Marc with Sister Madeline,' Gerard beamed. 'He was sobbing his heart out. *Oh Sister Madeline, I'm so sad. I don't like it here. Jae was really sweet and special. Nobody loves me. I can't stand it any more. I want to run away. Boo, hoo, hoo!*'

A few nervous laughs erupted as sets of eyeballs turned on Marc.

'You're so full of shit,' Marc tutted. 'I might have moaned a bit when she put the iodine on my cuts, but no way was I crying.'

'You looked like you'd been crying when I passed you on the stairs earlier,' Jacques noted.

'*I need to get out of here,*' Gerard teased. '*I'm so worthless. I can't stand my life any more.*'

Marc could see that most of the room believed Gerard's version of events and the pressure not to admit weakness felt like a vice crushing his head. Under normal circumstances he would have settled it by planting his fist in Gerard's face, but right now he wasn't even sure he could stand up straight, let alone fight.

To make matters worse, Lanier sensed that Marc was now on the back foot and moved in for the kill.

'You're such a girl, Kilgour,' Lanier said, rushing back towards Marc's bed. 'Remember at Easter, the last time Tomas really caned into you? You were practically crying then. And you were going on with this big rant about how you were gonna get Tomas back and how you were gonna run away. But nothing happened, because you're all mouth.'

'I've thought about running,' Marc said. 'You never know, I just might some day.'

'Full of crap,' Lanier shouted. 'Stick to crying for Sister Madeline.'

Everyone laughed except Marc and his loyal bunkmate Jacques.

'We've all thought about getting out of here,' Jacques said. 'But there's no point running away. Everyone gets busted and Tomas batters them and puts them on bread and water.'

'I know that,' Lanier said. 'But it's the way Marc goes on about it all the time, like he's some Mr Big or something.'

'You're lucky I'm injured, Lanier,' Marc shouted. 'Remember when you were down in the grass begging me to stop pounding your weak arse?'

'I'll fight you right now,' Lanier shouted, as he clambered over the mattresses.

A couple of jeers went up and Jacques summed up the mood. '*I* could beat Marc up, the state he's in at the moment.'

But the other boys backed away as Lanier crawled across the mattresses. He ended up kneeling across the tiny gap between Marc's bunk and the next with his fists bunched. Marc was in no state to fight, but Lanier clearly wasn't in the mood to show mercy.

As Lanier wound up his first punch, Marc kicked out. His foot connected with enough force to knock Lanier off balance, while at the same moment he grabbed the frame of his bunk and threw his weight to one side with enough force to shift the metal bed off its feet and several centimetres to one side.

It wasn't much, but it was enough to dislodge Lanier and he crashed helplessly into the narrow gap between beds, his knees hitting the floorboards with a bang.

'I'll kill you,' Lanier screamed, scrambling up as Jacques dived away in fright. Marc kicked out at Lanier's head, but it was only a glancing blow and before Marc knew it Lanier had grabbed his ankle and twisted it around painfully before dragging him down on to Jacques' bunk.

'Now you're mine,' Lanier smiled, as he swung his knee over Marc's waist.

Marc would have dodged easily if he'd been fit, but his body ached from the caning and before he knew it Lanier had his shoulder pinned to the mattress.

'Now what you gonna do?' Lanier gloated, as he slammed Marc's nose with his fist.

Marc wriggled, but couldn't break free as hard punches rained on his face and chest.

'Leave him!' Jacques shouted, as he bravely tried to pull Lanier off.

But suddenly everything in the attic room seemed to be vibrating and there was an increasingly loud droning sound outside. As curious boys rushed towards the window, Lanier was distracted. Marc brought up both knees and managed to free an arm.

A burst of machine-gun fire ripped across the front of

the orphanage and was followed by a huge explosion out on the road.

'Stuka dive bomber!' someone shouted.

The building shook as Marc and Lanier rolled uneasily away from each other. The other boys were all crowded around the window looking out back.

'It's on fire,' someone shouted. 'Coming right for us!'

Marc was startled as stricken boys raced over, under and between the bunks towards the staircase, which was already crowded with kids from the other attic bedroom who'd acted faster. As the orphanage roof continued to shudder, dust wafted down from creaking joists above Marc's head.

There were screams on the overcrowded staircase and the oil lamps in the hallway swung violently as the wooden frame of the orphanage lurched half a metre, tilting several frightened boys down the staircase.

After a few seconds in complete darkness, Marc looked down and saw that he was the last boy in the bedroom, apart from a tearful three year old who'd wandered from the next room in a state of panic.

'Come on, mate,' Marc said, scooping the toddler into his aching arms and edging painfully through the darkness towards the chaos on the staircase. Boys had fallen on top of one another when the building had shaken and the tangle of arms and legs on the landing was worsened by desperate boys trying to escape by scrabbling over them.

The building lurched once again and this time several windows shattered. The cracking of glass was instantly followed by a colossal bang and a wave of heat and light that sucked all the moisture out of the air. The toddler's fingers dug into the welts on Marc's back as the oil lamps dimmed, whilst desperate screams and a grey haze rose up the stairwell.

CHAPTER SIX

Paul nodded obediently as he moved his hands into a surrender position.

'Good boy,' the German said, smiling coldly. He was a slim man with small black eyes and he reeked of the tonic he used to slick down his hair. 'How many are in the house?'

'Three,' Paul mumbled.

'Who are the others?'

'My dad and my sister.'

'And your father is Digby Clarke?'

Paul nodded as the German let him up off the bed, but kept the gun in his face.

'Call your father in here. Try anything and I'll stick a bullet in your head.'

'Dad!'

The shout didn't appear to have any effect and the German narrowed his eyes. 'Again.'

'*Dad!*' Paul shouted, close to tears. 'I need you right now.'

But Rosie came in first. 'Dad's busy. What's the matter, squirt?'

Then she saw the German and the gun and screamed.

'*Silence!*' the German snarled.

'Will you two stop fighting,' Mr Clarke shouted impatiently as he moved down the hallway. 'I'm sick of—'

'Don't come in,' Rosie shouted, causing the German to turn his aim on her. But it was only a short walk from the kitchen and Mr Clarke had entered the doorway almost before the words were out. His anger turned to shock.

'Digby, old bean, what a delight,' the German smiled, switching from accented French to fairly dreadful English. 'I believe we met once before, in Monsieur Mannstein's office.'

'Briefly.' Clarke nodded, trying to create an impression of confidence to reassure his children.

'Where are the documents you stole from the German government?'

Mr Clarke shrugged innocently. 'I believe you're

mistaking me for someone else.'

'Oh, do you think so?' the German said sarcastically, as he pointed the gun down towards Paul's shoe. 'Perhaps your memory will function better *after* your son has a hole in his foot?'

Paul wasn't the bravest kid in the world and his stomach felt like someone was using it to churn butter.

'I just brought the papers in with me,' Mr Clarke said. 'They're in my briefcase.'

'Very good. Show them to me,' the German smiled, 'but keep your hands where I can see them.'

Mr Clarke backed into the hallway and began walking towards the living room.

'Follow your father,' the German ordered, gesturing towards the door with the end of his gun.

Paul felt horribly small as he stepped through to the living room. Mr Clarke picked his briefcase up from the rug and rested it atop a small table to open it. Rosie stepped up to a long sofa and the German nodded that it was OK for her to sit down. Paul sat at the opposite end.

Meanwhile, Mr Clarke had sprung the catches on his briefcase.

'Don't open it,' the German barked nervously. 'Turn the case towards me, then place one hand on your head.'

Paul noticed Rosie's hand creep towards the open

front of her father's bureau. He worried she'd get shot and wished she'd just sit still and do what she was told for once.

'Now,' the German said, addressing Mr Clarke, 'with your free hand, open the case. *Slowly*.'

Mr Clarke raised the lid and the German smiled slightly as he stepped up. Paul saw that the case was full of manila folders, similar to the ones he'd stacked up in the back of the car.

The German kept the gun on Mr Clarke as he moved closer to the case. But his expression wilted as he flipped through the folders.

'There are no blueprints here,' the German said. 'Where are the rest of the papers?'

Mr Clarke acted mystified. 'This is all I have. I don't know of any blueprints.'

The German swung the gun around and shouted, 'Which one of your children would you like me to kill first?'

Paul stared at his knees with a cushion clutched tightly to his side, but Rosie eyeballed the German defiantly.

'Maybe after I've killed you and your son, my colleagues and I can have some fun with your daughter,' the German smiled. 'She's feisty!'

Mr Clarke didn't rise to the twisted threat and tried to sound sincere. 'Sir, I truly don't know of any other papers.'

'Liar,' the German shouted, as the main door of the

apartment – which had been left ajar – moved with a slight kick.

A frail voice came from behind it. 'Monsieur Clarke? I heard shouting . . .'

The gun fired and Paul hollered as the bullet smashed into Madame Mujard's face. The impact killed the frail concierge instantly and the bullet exited the back of her skull, hitting the hallway wall with chunks of brain and skull for company.

The German baulked when he saw his elderly victim and Rosie sensed an opening. She leaped off the sofa and jammed her father's brass letter opener into the soft flesh just below his ribcage. The German stumbled forwards and collapsed on to the suitcase. Mr Clarke grabbed his arm and twisted the gun out of his hand.

'Rosie, grab the briefcase,' Mr Clarke ordered, tightening the German's arm behind his back.

Once the case was out of the way, Mr Clarke pressed the gun into the German's left shoulder blade and shot him. After passing through the German's torso, the bullet hit the single column supporting the table, tearing out a chunk of wood and making it snap. As the German hit the rug, Clarke stepped back with the gun at arm's length and fired a second shot into his temple.

'One in the heart, one in the head,' Clarke explained

as he picked up the far corner of the rug and threw it over the German's body. Then he looked up at Rosie and tried to smile. 'That was fantastic, sweetheart. You saved our bacon.'

But Rosie had tears in her eyes and Paul held on to the cushion as if his life depended on it. Nothing in their lives so far had prepared them for blood, brains and two dead bodies in their living room.

'What's going on, Dad?' Rosie sobbed, as she shook her head with disbelief. '*What* just happened?'

'I'll explain in the car,' Mr Clarke said stiffly. He didn't want to sound so harsh, but he didn't know how else to deal with the situation. 'You both trust me, don't you?' he asked. 'You know I wouldn't have killed a man unless I really had to?'

Rosie nodded, but Paul remained mute, his lips turning slightly blue.

'Snap out of it, son,' Mr Clarke said, as he snatched the cushion from Paul and shook him by the shoulders.

'What now?' Rosie asked, as her father dragged Madame Mujard into the apartment and shut the door.

'We've got to leave,' Clarke said. 'If someone heard that shot they'll fetch the police. Run into your rooms and grab your stuff. We're leaving in *two* minutes.'

'But I'm covered in blood,' Rosie protested. 'I need a wash.'

Mr Clarke groaned with frustration as he tucked the German's gun inside his jacket and walked towards the bureau. 'Rosie, I don't know about you, but I don't fancy being locked in a police cell when the German artillery starts blasting the city. So give yourself a quick wipe down if you have to, but that's it. Once you've got your things, there's a paper bag with some food for the journey on the kitchen table – make sure you grab that before we leave. I've got my travelling bag in the car already, but I want you to go in my room and fetch my gold cufflinks and your mother's jewellery box.'

'Right.' Rosie nodded loyally. But she sounded a touch put out as she rubbed her wet eyes. 'Aren't you going to help?'

Clarke shook his head as his hand hovered over the telephone. 'I've got to call a colleague. He has connections inside the Paris police and with luck he'll be able to smooth this mess over.'

As the children rushed off to change and pack, Mr Clarke got an operator to connect him with the British Embassy.

'Embassy main switchboard,' said the woman on the other end.

'I need to speak with Charles Henderson in section E,' Mr Clarke said.

'I'm sorry, sir, but Mr Henderson is no longer at the

Embassy and I don't believe he'll be coming back. The only staff who haven't been evacuated are myself, the Ambassador and two military attachés.'

'Damn and blast,' Mr Clarke growled. 'What about Henderson's secretary, Miss McAfferty? Can you get me her new number in London?'

'I might be able to find it, but I don't think there would be much point. All phone lines between France and Britain have been down since yesterday afternoon. We're communicating by radio only.'

Mr Clarke was exasperated. 'OK,' he gasped. 'If you do see Henderson, tell him that there's been a spot of bother at my apartment, but that I'm going to head south as planned.'

'I think it unlikely I'll see him, but I'll certainly try,' the receptionist said. 'Good day, sir.'

'Keep safe,' Mr Clarke said, as he put down the receiver and stood up. 'Come on, kids,' he shouted. 'Action stations.'

A few moments later Paul emerged from his bedroom wearing a shirt and long trousers that made him look like a proper French boy. He was clutching a small suitcase and a satchel crammed with comic books and art supplies. He still looked horribly shaken and if there had been time Mr Clarke would have given him a hug.

'We'll get through this, champ,' Clarke said, tousling

his son's hair, acutely aware that his gesture was inadequate.

Rosie emerged from the kitchen holding the bag of food. 'I stuffed everyone's clean clothes into the big case, but it's too heavy for me to lift down the stairs. I grabbed the photo albums and your camera, too.'

'Good thinking.' Mr Clarke smiled, as he waved his children towards the front door before grabbing his briefcase with one hand and the large suitcase with the other.

Trying to avoid the sight of the two bloodied bodies just a metre from his feet, Paul stepped into the corridor outside.

Rosie had lived in apartment sixteen since she was five years old. She felt sad as she pulled closed the door for what was surely the last time.

Paul finally broke his silence as he chased his father and sister down the narrow staircase. 'Dad, are you a spy or something?'

CHAPTER SEVEN

There were a few knocks, a couple of sprains and one nun with a broken arm beneath the boys piled up on the landing, but the orphanage had survived its brush with annihilation. The stricken German dive bomber had clipped the roof, shattering chimney pots and dislodging a chunk of brickwork. A great pile of rubble had clattered down the chimney, causing clouds of dust and ash to erupt from all the fireplaces on the east side of the house.

In wintertime burning embers would have blown across every floor of the house, but luckily it was summer. The fireplaces were dormant and the only blaze was caused by an oil lamp coming down from its hook and spilling across the floor. The flames were extinguished by two quick-thinking boys, who smothered them with a mattress.

Marc and his tiny companion were amongst the last to get out of the ash and dust. They both coughed as they stepped into a sunset made even more dramatic by towers of flame erupting in two directions on the horizon.

The German Stuka had been one of hundreds zigzagging across the countryside that evening, scouring the roads for convoys of French soldiers and equipment. After passing the orphanage, the stricken aeroplane had torn apart the neighbouring barn, its flaming engine setting fire to the vegetable store and the chicken coops inside. It finally crashed in the field beyond, coming to a halt in a deep furrow before the flames ignited its remaining cargo of bombs, incinerating the pilot and throwing up tonnes of earth as every building within a kilometre shuddered.

A hundred metres in the other direction, two French army trucks bombed by the Stuka were ablaze and a third had lost its rear axle when the blast threw its back end off the road and several metres into the air.

Soldiers – some badly burned – were staggering across the front lawn, whilst nuns and some of the older boys rushed their way offering help. The younger boys had divided amongst gawpers who'd run out into the field beyond the orphanage to study the crater left by the aircraft and a smaller group who'd begun rounding up chickens, which had done a remarkable job of escaping the flames.

As Marc set the toddler on the grass, he noticed Director Tomas rushing from his small cottage on the west side of the orphanage.

'Is everyone OK?' Tomas asked, before shielding his eyes from the low sun and glancing upwards at the damaged chimney. He then charged into the building, almost knocking down a nun who was carrying out rags and a bucket of water to attend to the burn victims.

Seeing the director reminded Marc that he was hungry. Tomas lived alone in his cottage and supplemented the basic fare served to orphans with goodies delivered from a delicatessen in Beauvais.

Marc glanced around before striding purposefully towards the cottage. The walk took less than a minute and while it seemed unlikely that the director would return home in the midst of the present crisis, his heart started to bang. As far as he knew, no boy had ever dared to enter Tomas' cottage and two beatings in one day would be more than his body could take.

If you were the kind of person who liked dinky little cottages, you might have found the director's home pretty. Its white exterior was immaculate – repainted every summer by two teenagers who would be thrashed if they did a poor job – and Tomas gave his garden the kind of love and attention that he unfailingly spared the orphans. But Marc was only impressed by the great ocean liners and office towers he saw in comics and magazines. The cottage was just a quaint symbol of the countryside that he was determined to leave the instant he got the chance.

The front door was ajar and Marc craned his neck inside before stepping on to the uneven stone floor. The cottage was no more than six paces in either direction and the single ground-floor room had a kitchen range, a sink and a few cabinets on one side in front of a leaded window that had cracked in the blast. There was a dining table in the centre and on the opposite side a cosy space with two armchairs and a bookcase with a radio standing on top. Stairs at the rear led to the upstairs room and they were so narrow that the director must have had to turn sideways to climb them.

All Marc's life the director had been like a god, with the unquestionable power to withhold food and inflict pain. Yet seeing the humble cottage reminded Marc that the director of a rural orphanage was not a president or a general; not even a landowner like Morel, or a respected figure within the local area such as the priest. This realisation of Director Tomas' insignificance was liberating and Marc felt more confident as he opened the larder cabinet, to be confronted by all manner of food.

His eyes dashed excitedly over things he'd never tasted: sardines and tinned orange segments, goose pâté, olives, a plate of chicken wings and a jar of honey. Marc didn't want to risk getting caught inside the house so he grabbed a clean cloth from the lower shelf and laid it flat on the draining board before piling it with bread, chicken, a lump of cheese and a dollop of pâté scooped out with his finger. He was desperate to try the oranges, but he'd never opened a tin can and had no idea how to do it.

As Marc picked up the tins to see what might be underneath he came to a slightly rusted tin that had originally contained salt. As he raised it up he heard the unmistakeable jangle of coins. Curious, he unscrewed the lid and saw that amidst the coins was a thick bundle of notes, mostly the fifty- and one-hundred-franc variety.

The sight of money was intoxicating, but if Marc took it – or even *some* of it – he'd be found out the moment he walked into the village's only shop waving a fifty-franc note. He replaced the tin, gathered up the food in the cloth and hurried outside.

He walked around to the back of the director's home and brushed a couple of wood-pigs aside before sitting on the stump of a felled tree. It was a good vantage point from which he could easily take cover if anyone approached the cottage.

After spreading the cloth in his lap, Marc jumped with fright as a distant explosion lit up the scene. Another Stuka rose vertically out of its dive, its tiny silhouette leaving a trail in the purple sky.

Following the fright he bit greedily into the bread and the chicken wings. Then he delved into the pâté, swallowed the sardines – which he found too salty but ate anyway – and lastly gorged on the miniature cheese, which came from a local farm. The tang of its runny centre burst into his mouth when he bit through the rubbery crust.

The food was richer than Marc was used to and its illicit nature, combined with hunger and the moody setting, made it spectacular. It was almost enough to make him forget the pain in his thigh and the stinging welts down his back.

When he finished, Marc licked his fingertips and realised he was thirsty. The golden sunset of ten minutes earlier was now just a purple fringe above the tree line. As he crept back towards Tomas' cottage he noticed the brand new bike resting against the side of the house and did some instant maths:

BIKE + MONEY = FREEDOM

Marc had lived his entire twelve years in the

orphanage and had never ventured further than the nearest village and neighbouring farms, except for one five-night stay in the Beauvais infirmary, which he barely remembered because he'd been delirious with a severe case of measles.

The bike and the money were his best ever chance to escape, but running away would be the biggest decision of Marc's life and just considering it made him breathless.

Impossibly excited, Marc looked around to make sure that he was still alone before stepping back into the cottage. He filled a glass with tap water and drained it in four huge gulps while questions bubbled in his head.

Marc was no fantasist. Running away would be hard. At twelve years old he was sure to be caught eventually and returned to Director Tomas for multiple beatings, a week on bread and water and months sleeping in the unheated barn – assuming it was rebuilt in time.

On the other hand he could barely stand the thought of another night crammed in the hot attic room, with the constant pressure to act tough while lads fought the same tedious battles. All his life he'd wanted to go on a train, spend a night under the stars, steal eggs from a chicken coop and ride the lift to the top of the Eiffel Tower . . .

The war, however, was a severe complication. He'd heard that many roads were badly damaged, although that was much less of a problem for a bicycle than a truck.

And what would happen if the Germans got him, rather than the French police? Then again, would it be any better if he waited around until the Germans reached the orphanage? And maybe if he got far enough south they'd never get him at all. But then where would he go? Would there be anyone to give him food and put a roof over his head once the money ran out?

Marc stepped towards the larder cupboard. He opened the door and stared at the old salt tin with the director's savings inside, as every question he asked himself spawned two more. He knew he'd never be able to answer all – or even most – of them. He realised there was only one question that really mattered:

Do I have the guts to run away, or am I all mouth like Lanier says I am?

Marc thought about fate. Perhaps god had left the bicycle and money as a temptation, to see if he would steal them. Or, maybe god wanted him to take the decision to leave? He decided to reach into the tin and pull out a single coin without looking. If it came up heads when he opened his palm he would leave. If it came up tails he would stay.

It seemed stupid, but it was the only plan Marc had. He dashed back to the door of the cottage for a final look to make sure nobody was coming. Then he unscrewed the tin and grabbed a coin blindly. He could hardly bear to open his fist.

Marc trembled as he released his fingers and saw the buckled two-cent piece with the face of Liberty staring at him. He reached into the tin and grabbed the rest of the director's savings.

CHAPTER EIGHT

Mr Clarke drove quickly with Rosie in the front and Paul in the back with the luggage piled around him. Concerned that the police were coming, or that another German agent might be waiting outside, they hadn't wasted time packing the boot.

'I owe the pair of you an apology,' Clarke said, once they'd caught their breath and put a couple of kilometres between themselves and the apartment. 'You never should have had to see that. If it was up to me you'd be safe and sound in England right now. Imperial Wireless offered to help pay your school fees after your mother died, but because she was French she never liked the idea of you two going to an English boarding school.'

Paul was in shock, and struggling to reconcile his

father's warm persona with his calculating behaviour back at the apartment. 'So who was that German?' he asked.

'Abwehr – German secret service.'

'But Mujard said the French police came too,' Rosie noted.

'No,' Clarke said, shaking his head as the Citroën turned right into a cobbled alleyway. It was a poor neighbourhood and strands of washing hung from the apartment blocks on either side of them. 'German agents have been operating in Paris for years, but since the invasion they've become quite brazen. They've taken to disguising themselves as police officers and their enemies have been disappearing, either shot or kidnapped and smuggled out for interrogation. Henderson reckons the French police are turning a blind eye.'

'Why?' Paul asked.

'A lot of police officers have gone south. Those who've stayed behind hope to be working for the Germans in a few weeks' time and have no intention of antagonising their future bosses.'

'Who is this Henderson?' Rosie asked. 'A spy?'

Mr Clarke nodded. 'He works for a branch of naval intelligence called the Espionage Research Unit. It's a small department that specialises in unearthing enemy technology.'

'And you work as a spy too?'

Clarke laughed at the thought. 'I went on an intelligence corps training course back when I was in the navy, but it's certainly not my day job. I first met Henderson about four years ago. As well as standard radios like we have in the apartment, Imperial Wireless makes specialist equipment like radios for military aircraft and ships, directional beacons, scrambler systems and such like.

'I've been selling that equipment into France for seventeen years and over that time I've got to know everyone in the business – from the officers in the French naval procurement office, all the way down to the admin staff in our rivals' sales offices.

'Every few months Henderson and I meet for a drink. He's always interested in the latest technical developments from our rivals and—'

Clarke had to stop speaking because he'd turned into a road that was blocked off by wooden barriers. They were less than a hundred metres away from a major railway station and the courtyard in front of it was jammed with people. But the steps leading inside were cordoned off and soldiers stood at wrought-iron gates with their guns poised.

A flat-capped policeman strode importantly towards the car as Mr Clarke wound down his window.

'Do you have reservations for a train?' he asked curtly.

Clarke shook his head. 'I'm just trying to get across town.'

The officer shrugged before dramatically pointing him back the way he'd come. 'No access. Leave at once!'

'Blast,' Clarke said, as the front tyre scraped the kerb. 'Rosie, pull the map from under the seat and work out another way out of the city.'

After a few hundred metres Mr Clarke pulled up outside a laundry and leaned across to study the map his daughter had unfurled in her lap. He'd travelled all over France, persuading department stores to stock Imperial Wireless radios, so he knew the roads well and it took less than half a minute to familiarise himself with an alternative route.

Once he was back on roads he knew, Mr Clarke continued his story.

'Late last year I got wind of a new transceiver – that's a radio set that transmits and receives – designed and built by a Frenchman called Luc Mannstein. He runs a family company that has made very expensive and very beautiful watches for more than two hundred years. But Mannstein is also a keen radio amateur. Like a lot of hobbyists he'd built his own radio equipment and aerials that could transmit all over the world; but things only got interesting when he decided to apply his skills as a watchmaker to the production of a miniature set.

'Mannstein has designed and built a powerful and robust radio transceiver that is less than a third of the weight of anything we make at IWC. Even with an aerial, a battery and a Morse key or microphone it can be comfortably carried in a leather pouch strapped to your chest. At present there are only a few hand-built prototypes in existence, but if the design could be mass produced it would revolutionise communications.'

Mr Clarke began to sound like his usual self again as he broke into a salesman's patter. 'I mean, imagine a radio small and light enough to be carried by every soldier on the battlefield, or every police officer on his beat. Instant communication! Car drivers could radio one another to announce accidents or traffic jams. Some day it's even possible that husbands could radio their wives in the kitchen to say that they're on their way home from work.'

'And that's what all these documents are, isn't it?' Paul said, as he eyed the stack of papers on the seat beside him. 'Plans for Mannstein's miniature transceiver.'

'That's right,' Mr Clarke said. 'You see, in the longer term the compact radio might be a mass-market product, but the Espionage Research Unit is interested in its covert applications. If you're working as a spy behind enemy lines you need a transceiver that is small, light and tough.

'As soon as I found out about Mannstein's miniature set I told my bosses at IWC. They made Mannstein an offer to buy into his company and build a workshop in which to begin producing radios. Unfortunately IWC has been hammered by American imports and we've had a few tough years financially. Our offer was far from spectacular and Mannstein rejected it.

'By this time Henderson had spoken to the British Government about the potential of Mannstein's design and he was trying to get some money together to up the bid. Unfortunately the whole thing got bogged down in red tape just as the Germans entered the bidding.

'The Nazis' attitude is to spend whatever it takes to acquire the best technology available. So while the French Government totally ignored the situation and the British fudged over whether it was right to interfere in the free market, the Germans came in with a gold-plated offer: more money, a brand new factory in Germany and a state of the art research facility where Mannstein could refine his technology.

'Once the Germans were involved the British upped their bid, but it still wasn't a patch on the German offer. Mannstein was all set to sign a deal and move his company to Germany, but at the last moment France declared war and the whole thing collapsed.'

'So he signed the deal with Britain?'

Mr Clarke shook his head. 'The French wouldn't allow that either. It all got bogged down in a row over export licences. They even confiscated Mannstein's passport in case he tried to leave the country. Mannstein's company didn't have enough money to mass produce the radio by itself and the whole project has been in limbo for nine months.

'When the success of the German invasion shocked the hell out of everyone, I spoke to Henderson again and we set up an emergency meeting in Mannstein's office. We were going to offer him safe passage to Britain, but when I got there I walked into the reception and bumped into our German friend from the apartment, along with two of his colleagues.

'Mannstein wasn't too pleased to see us. He didn't say much, but I got the impression that he thought we'd messed him around too much in the past and he would be happy to sit back and wait for the Germans to invade so that he could work with them.

'When I left with Henderson I mentioned that I knew a young salesman who worked in Mannstein's office – I'd put in a good word for him back when I was on friendly terms with Mannstein and helped him land the job. As luck would have it the young fellow is a Jew and he was desperate to head south before the Boche arrived. I caught up with him just before he quit and left town with his family.

'He let me copy his keys to Mannstein's office and workshop. I got up at three a.m. this morning and drove over there. The security system was virtually non-existent, but unfortunately our German friends were expecting us. As I was coming back to my car with the documents they jumped me. Luckily I had my knife at the ready and I managed to stab one and knock the other out.'

Rosie and Paul shared an incredulous glance. They were both impressed and shocked by their father's story. With his flamboyant dress and soft manner he'd never struck them as the type of man who kept a knife at the ready.

'If I'd done things by the book I would have killed them both,' Mr Clarke went on. 'But I *didn't*, which was a damned fool thing because they knew who I was and that almost led to them killing all three of us back in the apartment.'

As Mr Clarke said this he turned and smiled at his daughter. 'But you saved us, sweetheart.'

Rosie shook her head. 'Not before he killed Madame Mujard though.'

'No,' Mr Clarke said, nodding solemnly. 'That terrible murder was my fault, and it was totally unacceptable to put you two in such danger too.'

'Don't keep apologising,' Paul said. 'You did your best.'

Mr Clarke smiled wryly. Paul never spoke much, but that only made his words count for more when he did. 'All I know is that if your mother's up there watching over us, I'd be fairly certain that right now she's standing with her hands on her hips wishing she could yell at me.'

CHAPTER NINE

Marc wheeled the director's bike away from the cottage and kept low as he rushed through the field of wheat behind the orphanage. He had money, transport, a knife and a pigskin bag stolen from the director into which he'd stuffed tins of food and a can opener which he'd vowed to figure out later. Clothing, however, was still a problem.

Marc wore nothing but the blood-spattered shorts in which he'd emerged from bed. Fortunately the nuns were scrupulous in washing the orphans' ragged clothes, and shirts and trousers had been left to hang overnight on half a dozen crisscrossed washing lines. Everyone was on the opposite side of the house, either attending the wounded soldiers or forming part of the human chain passing buckets and saucepans of water to douse the blazing barn, so it was easy enough to strip trousers, under-shorts, socks and two white shirts from the line.

Shoes were trickier. Besides the stinking rubber boots he wore for mucking out the dairy shed, Marc only owned a pair of fifth-hand canvas plimsolls that were too small. He always threw them off and ran barefoot as soon as he was out of school, and they were completely unsuited to a long journey.

However, some of the older boys were apprenticed to work for local tradesmen and needed proper boots for their work. Marc had always coveted a pair of boots, especially in the winter, when bare feet or soggy canvas plimsolls were painfully cold. On the other hand, he didn't want to steal an older boy's boots, partly because the director would probably call the boy careless and beat him for losing them and partly because boots were about the most valuable thing any orphan owned. If Marc ever came back he'd have more than just the director to reckon with.

But Marc couldn't make it to Paris without something decent on his feet, so he didn't have much choice, and he raced into the orphanage. The dust that had blown out of the fireplaces had settled and it stuck to his damp soles as he ran up the stairs.

He'd planned to go all the way up to the attic, but he

could hear Tomas up there with two of the oldest boys. As he peered up the stairs he could see them standing in the hallway, inspecting the damaged chimney. If the director recognised the stolen pigskin bag slung over Marc's back his escape would come to an abrupt and painful end.

This meant he had to risk getting boots from the first floor. The orphans had dozens of rivalries, but the biggest was between boys who slept in the attic and boys who slept on the first floor. New arrivals assigned to one floor were immediately forced to run the gauntlet of the other, where they would be mercilessly kicked and punched as they tried to reach the brick wall at the far end of the corridor. Any boy who showed cowardice would be further battered by his own roommates.

Because the bedrooms were so crammed, boys had to shed their footwear in the doorways before entering. A few had returned for their boots, but there were still several pairs in the doorway of the first bedroom as Marc stepped inside.

He'd hoped everyone would be out, but a ten year old called Victor sat on his bunk, nursing an arm in a cast.

'Hey!' he shouted aggressively. 'Get off our floor, attic boy.'

Marc tried to think up some clever reason why he needed someone else's boots but there was no way around it. 'Mind your own business, cripple.'

Marc eyed the boots on the floor. They were all huge, except for one pair, which he knew belonged to a kid called Noel who was apprenticed to the local blacksmith. Marc grabbed the boots by their laces. This rankled, because Noel was one of the nicest kids in the orphanage.

'Put them back,' Victor said firmly, though he didn't come any closer because Marc was strong and had two arms to fight with.

'Fifty francs if you keep your trap shut,' Marc said, pulling a note out of his shorts.

Victor's eyes bulged when he saw the money and Marc thought he was going to take it, but Victor wasn't a fool. Fifty francs was only useful if there was somewhere to spend it and even the dumbest orphan knew that going into the village with that kind of cash would lead to an inquisition followed by a beating in the director's office.

'Put them down, now,' Victor said firmly. 'I'll tell the lads and you'll get such a kicking.'

Marc thought about beating Victor up. He reckoned he could do it easily enough, but there was bound to be yelling and the director was close enough to hear.

'Just tell Noel that I owe him one,' Marc said sadly, as he backed out of the room and swung the boots over his shoulder before jogging towards the stairs.

'Are you thick or something?' Victor screamed, jumping off his bed to give chase.

Marc was no slouch and Victor was two years younger, but the gash on his thigh slowed him down and Victor was right on his back as he reached the ground floor. Victor screamed out for help as Marc whizzed past the kitchen doorway. It arrived in the form of a sixteen-year-old roommate called Sebastien, who happened to be coming inside.

'He's nicked Noel's boots!' Victor shouted.

Marc almost ran straight into the teenager, but managed to spin on the ball of his foot and clatter into Victor, leaving him sprawled out at the bottom of the stairs. He landed awkwardly on his cast and moaned in pain.

Two French soldiers and a nun were blocking Marc from heading out the back, which left the kitchen as his only option. A half-conscious soldier with a chunk of shrapnel in his arm sat at the table as Marc ran in. There was no door, so he raced the length of the room and vaulted into the huge sink, where giant pots and pans used to cook for a hundred kids were scrubbed after each meal.

The window behind this sink was shut and Marc lost valuable time as he wrestled with a tight brass handle. As the bewildered soldier looked on, Marc swung the window outwards and jumped through.

The drop was less than a metre, but Marc's weakened leg buckled and the palm he put out to save himself hit the jagged edge of a stone. The pain made him gasp and by the time he'd found his feet Sebastien's frighteningly muscular torso was squeezing through the gap.

With his leg so weak, Marc knew he'd never make it to the field where he'd stashed the bike before the teenager caught up. His only chance would be if he attacked Sebastien while he was trapped in the window frame and, after briefly considering swinging at him with the boots, Marc realised that the window itself was the best weapon.

Sebastien saw what was going to happen and shouted out as Marc grabbed the window frame. With his hands trapped at his sides, there was nothing Sebastien could do as the pane of glass smashed over the top of his head.

Marc didn't stand around to gawp, but Sebastien sounded like he was in a lot of pain and beads of blood were welling around a large gash in his forehead. It wasn't a pretty sight and it scared the wits out of Marc. Five minutes earlier he could have ditched the director's money and backed out, but now there were stolen boots, panes of broken glass and one of the biggest kids in the orphanage needing his face stitched. There was no going back.

Luckily, everyone else was still around the front of the building and Marc had a clear run as he ducked through the washing towards the field. His hand and his thigh hurt badly and he stung in a dozen other places where he'd been caned, but adrenaline is a great painkiller and Marc's was flowing in buckets.

As he pushed himself through a low hedge into the field, he looked back at the orphanage and felt sick. Despite all the bad food, the noise, the heat, the beatings and the bullying, there was still part of him that wanted to be able to climb back on his bunk and fall asleep.

The hugeness of what Marc had committed himself to was all-consuming. He was at the most important turning point of his twelve years and, as he bent down to grab the bike, a great burst of acid erupted from his throat.

He wondered if he'd just made the biggest mistake of his life.

CHAPTER TEN

The orphans were allowed to use a tatty bicycle when they were sent to the village on an errand, but it was years since Marc had ridden it and the director's brand new Peugeot was a different beast: adult-sized, with decent brakes, three gears and the saddle set high. It took a few kilometres to get the feel of it but even then it wasn't a comfortable ride.

There was no traffic heading north and the bombed trucks prevented anything with four wheels coming along the road behind him, but he passed huddles of refugees every few hundred metres. The lucky ones had horses and carts. Those without used prams, or handcarts nailed together from scrap. Some were piled impossibly high with mattresses and pots and pans, while others served as platforms for sleeping children.

By the time Marc reached the village his eyes had adjusted to the darkness. His confidence in the saddle had grown and he'd worked out the value of having gears. The bakery at the edge of the village appeared to have caught a bomb blast and rubble had spilled into the road, but his face was known around here so he didn't slow down to look.

The cobbles in the village square made the bike shudder and Marc felt a rush of excitement as he followed a direction sign pointing at *Beauvais 5km*. The first part of this was a steep hill and, when he reached the brow, he decided that there was enough space between himself and the orphanage to risk making a stop.

Marc pulled into a shallow ditch at the roadside, mopping the sweat from his brow on to his bare arm as he stepped off the bike. He was short of breath and he regretted not bringing any water.

He sat on a hump in the dry grass and swapped his shorts for a white shirt, corduroy trousers, socks and finally the boots. He'd never worn proper boots before and his first steps were an exploration of their heaviness and the unyielding soles. They didn't seem a bad fit.

Although Marc was more comfortable barefoot, the boots were a thrill. They made him feel grown up and for a few moments he sensed freedom and excitement. But it wasn't long before he considered that someone might be after him and he quickly swung the pigskin over his back and straddled the bike for the journey downhill.

Marc had wanted to see Beauvais for as long as he could remember. It was a town of less than 50,000 people, but to a boy from nowhere the cathedral, the cinemas and the shops with handmade chocolates and cream cakes piled in the windows were the stuff of legend.

But the city was on the main invasion route heading towards Paris and the German air force's attempts to soften it up had turned Marc's dream into a nightmare. The final stretch of road into town was like hell, with the smell of burning fuel in the air and curls of smoke drifting across the face of the moon. The road was partially blocked by a crater with the remains of a car tilted into it. Charred trees at the roadside had been cut to make a clear path for traffic, but this ground was uneven and Marc was forced to dismount.

Marc wheeled his bike close to the road's edge and noticed a line of bodies covered with blankets or jackets. As if this wasn't spooky enough a huge rat scuttled across his path and cut into the trees. A glance into the crater exposed him to the shadowy outlines of rats and crows bickering over blood and intestines that had spilled when a body had been dragged away.

Completely revolted, Marc was hit by the reality of being alone. He'd just passed two elderly refugees wheeling pet birds and a ginger cat and he considered running back and begging them for help.

But realistically they were in no position to help anyone. Marc looked towards the black outline of Beauvais and contemplated turning back towards the orphanage. If a man important enough to own a smart car could end up with his guts spilled across the road, what chance did a twelve-year-old orphan have?

Trouble was, he had burned his bridges. He could just imagine Lanier and the others laughing their arses off when they heard that he'd run away, only to arrive back within the hour. And as for the reactions of Sebastien and Director Tomas . . .

Almost unconsciously, Marc picked up his heavy boots and pushed the bike towards Beauvais. Once he was past the crater he remounted and was soon cycling cautiously through dark streets with buildings close on either side. Most had their shutters closed for the night. All the lights were blacked out to prevent the city being picked out by German pilots, but several fires lingered from an earlier raid and explosions had shattered windows everywhere. Most of the glass had been swept into gutters, but it was still across the road in places and Marc feared a puncture.

Things became livelier as he freewheeled the bottom of a hill and turned on to one of the town's main boulevards. Like everywhere else in northern France, the population of Beauvais had split between those who'd fled south and those who'd abandoned themselves to whatever fate the Germans had in store.

The stay-behinds seemed determined to enjoy their last breath of freedom. The air was warm and the cafés whose owners had stayed in town were crammed with people. Although the street lanterns had been switched off and each café had black curtains or shutters drawn across the windows to keep out the light, Marc saw pinpricks of candlelight on the outdoor tables and the orange glow of cigarettes dancing expressively in the hands of people who'd had too much to drink.

The mass of chatter was nothing out of the ordinary for a street of bars and cafés, but Marc had never seen so many adults in one place before and their apparent ease in near black surroundings made him feel even more out of place.

He pulled up when he came to a horse trough with a drinking fountain mounted on the brick plinth behind it. After dropping the bike he leaned into the spout and gasped with relief as he gulped cool water.

'Change?' a man asked noisily, making Marc jump.

Water dribbled down Marc's chin as he backed away

from the fountain and eyed the old man. He wore only shorts and boots, but was so filthy that it took Marc a few seconds to realise that he wasn't in some kind of fancy-dress gorilla suit.

'Anything you can spare,' the man smiled, as he held out his hand. 'Just a few coins.'

As he said this, Marc caught a noseful of booze, sweat and puke. He scrambled backwards, stumbling over his bike before standing it up and riding on in a panic.

At the next junction Marc found a signpost pointing towards the train station. He knew it was approximately sixty kilometres to Paris and according to the railway map pinned up at his school there were trains to everywhere in France once you got there.

Marc suffered an emotional explosion as he rode around the corner and got his first glimpse of the place where his mother had abandoned him. The feeling was neither good nor bad, but it was powerful for the few moments until it turned into disappointment.

In Marc's imagination Beauvais station had always been a fantastic place, with engines venting steam under a wrought-iron roof, boys selling newspapers and the bustle of expensively-dressed people with places to go. But Beauvais was on a rural branch line and its station was merely two open platforms, with a ticket office, a waiting room and a café that looked as if it had been boarded up for some years.

The people were the same desperate souls that Marc had seen on the road. The more he saw of them, the more he realised that they were dregs. The lucky few who owned cars, those with decent carts and even those who were simply healthy enough to maintain a good walking pace had passed through days earlier.

Only the truly desperate washed up at Beauvais station hoping for a train. Many were elderly and those that weren't tended to be women with young children – sometimes as many as four or five spread around exhausted mothers like litters of pigs. Their men were either dead, fighting at the front, or imprisoned by the Germans.

Some people waited hopefully on the station platform, staring down the tracks as though the very act of looking might make the train come sooner. The ticket office was tiny so most sat in the street outside. Everyone was dirty and everywhere Marc looked he saw feet covered in vile scabs and blisters.

There was no queue at the ticket office, but the teenaged ticket officer had the weariness of someone who knew exactly what he was going to be asked.

'There are three trains up the line to the north,' the youth explained, as he whirled his cap around on his index finger. 'I can sell you a ticket, but I can't say if a train will come tonight, tomorrow or any other time. And when it does come I can't say if it will stop, or if there will be space to board. The last train was three hours back. It was packed with injured troops and the driver didn't stop.'

Marc nodded solemnly. 'When will you know if a train is coming?'

'All our telephones to the north are down. The stationmaster gets an automatic warning when a train reaches the water tower just up the line, but you'll most likely have heard it coming by then anyway.'

Marc had led a sheltered life. He'd always imagined trains as huge invulnerable beasts. It hadn't occurred to him that one bomb-damaged rail was all it took to bring a hundred kilometres of track to a standstill. He was visibly upset and the teenager took pity.

'Are you alone?' the lad asked.

Marc nodded. He thought about justifying himself by making up a background story about how his mother had been killed, but with regular bombings and streams of refugees on the road a twelve year old travelling alone was nothing out of the ordinary.

'Is your bike any good?'

'Fine,' Marc said.

The young ticket officer smiled. 'Why don't you ride? Paris is less than sixty kilometres. If you set off now and keep a steady pace you'll reach the outskirts by morning.'

Marc looked uncertain. 'I have money. Is there a place in town I could rest? Then I could set off once it gets light.'

'Your choice.' The ticket collector shrugged. 'But the German air force is targeting the main roads. They're less active at night and you can take cover more easily if they do come at you.'

It was ten o'clock and Marc would normally be in bed by now, but after the craziest day of his life he reckoned he'd be unlikely to sleep even if he tried.

'Is it easy?' Marc asked. 'I mean, I won't get lost or anything?'

'It's Paris, for the lord's sake,' the ticket officer said, smirking. 'The road leads straight there. You just ride back down towards the river and turn right. Within a few minutes you'll come to the edge of town and a three-way fork. You take the middle road. There's no mistaking it because it's wider than the others. Then it's basically a straight ride all the way to Paris.'

'Great.' Marc smiled. 'Thanks so much for your help.'

Marc wheeled the bike away from the ticket counter and headed back to the street. He was daunted by the prospect of such a long ride, but as he looked at the pitiful humans around the station he realised that with money, a bike and decent health on his side he was much better off than any of them.

He was touched by pity as he pedalled away, but he also drew satisfaction from the sense that he wasn't on the bottom of the pile. It took a painful twinge from his thigh to prick this bubble. His leg had been OK on the journey from the orphanage, but he wondered anxiously if it would stand an all-night ride.

After clearing the station, Marc decided to buy something to drink. No shops were open this late, so he took a left and headed back towards the cafés.

There seemed to be little difference between one café and another, so Marc stopped at the first and wheeled his bike towards the entrance. The circular tables outside were packed tight and while a couple of ladies pulled in their chairs to let him between the first set, a man sitting with his boots on the next table tutted and shooed him away with his hand.

Marc was perturbed, but he was spotted by a waitress holding a tray of beers and she came over to ask what he wanted.

'Just some water for a journey,' he explained, as he pulled out a ten-franc note. 'I'm cycling to Paris.'

The waitress told him to wait and after dropping off the beers she came back holding a large mineral water bottle with a screw-on cap.

'How much?' Marc asked, as he realised that another

of his weaknesses was that he had little idea of what things cost.

'It's on the house for a sweet boy like you,' the waitress said warmly.

As Marc took the cool bottle and smiled gratefully a great roar of laughter went up from the table beside him.

'He's a bit young for one of your toy boys, Sabine,' a drunken man jeered.

'Would you fancy a roll in the sack with her, kid?' his companion teased, as he reached out and grabbed the attractive waitress's bum.

'Thank you, miss,' Marc said, trying to ignore the remarks.

'Leave him be,' Sabine said, as she cuffed one of the drunks around the head. 'You're embarrassing the poor kid.'

The laughter dried up as an orange flash erupted in the distance, followed by three thumps that set ripples through the glasses of beer on the table.

'Bloody hell,' the waitress said, as she looked over her shoulder towards the light. 'Sounded more like artillery that time.' Then she looked at Marc again. 'You ride safe, OK? And say hello to Paris for me.'

'Thank you,' Marc said for what felt like at least the sixth time, as he pulled open the draw-string of his bag and placed the bottle inside, nestled between a cloth and his dirty shorts so that it didn't break.

After backing the bike out, he gave a quick wave as he pedalled off. When he turned to face the road he noticed a soldier just a few metres ahead.

'Coming through,' Marc shouted, swerving to avoid the scruffy figure. His chest was bare beneath a muddy army jacket and Marc guessed he was drunk.

But as Marc pedalled by the soldier kicked out. The bike clattered over and Marc's knee banged hard on the stone as the soldier pounced on top and slapped him across the mouth.

'Stay down,' the soldier ordered, shaking his fist in Marc's face as he ripped the bike away.

Marc was less than twenty metres from the café and the waitress and the two men who'd teased him came running. But by the time they arrived the soldier was pedalling off into the night.

'Are you all right, son?' one of the men asked, as he gave Marc a hand up.

He'd taken a nasty blow in the mouth and gasped with pain when he put weight on his knee.

'Damn nice bike that, too,' the other drunk noted, as he picked Marc's bag off the ground.

Marc tried not to cry as they helped him hobble towards the café, but he already had a tear streaking down his cheek.

'Looks like a nasty cut,' the waitress said. 'Better bring him inside and I'll clean it up.'

CHAPTER ELEVEN

The first stretch out of Paris was a crawl, but the hard work really started when the Citroën joined up with the main road heading south. Mr Clarke had hoped to travel 120 kilometres to Orléans and then stop overnight with an old friend who was a buyer at the town's department store.

Clarke had the advantage of a car, and the thousands of kilometres he'd driven as a salesman for Imperial Wireless had left him with excellent knowledge of France's back roads. But the refugees formed an impenetrable mass of slow-moving carts and bodies. Driving through them was agonising – constantly stopping and starting, rarely managing to break out of first gear and, in spots where the road narrowed, the car was actually a disadvantage. A blast of the horn achieved nothing and he had to use the car to physically push people aside. This was easily overdone and arguments regularly flared between drivers and foot-sloggers.

The Citroën suffered small attacks – from people pounding it with fists and boots or scratching the paint with keys. In one instance a man whose daughter suffered a painful knock from the front bumper ripped off a door mirror. Fearing that he would smash a window next, Clarke placed a hand on the gun he'd seized from the German, but luckily the man hurled the mirror into a hedge and backed off in a volley of foul language.

Paul knew he was in the midst of something extraordinary. He grabbed a pad from his satchel and made quick sketches of refugees, overloaded carts and bombed cottages. Alarmingly, he kept seeing cars similar to their own that had succumbed to slow driving and warm weather and blown their radiators.

While Paul withdrew into himself Rosie did the opposite, and constantly expressed pity as she gave a running commentary on some of the more pathetic refugees. There were people on crutches, people so old that they could barely walk; while the dead and unconscious littered the sides of the road. A few casualties were the result of air raids, but most had simply collapsed after walking hundreds of kilometres, laden with possessions.

'Enough,' Mr Clarke said finally, after his daughter noticed a British serviceman with his arm in a sling amidst the crowd. 'I *can* see! I have eyes! I can't think straight with your constant babbling.'

Rosie sulked, crossing her arms and staring directly ahead. After a few minutes of defiance she opened the door and got into the back beside Paul. When it started getting dark they pulled the curtains in the spacious rear compartment and arranged the luggage so that they could put their feet up. It wasn't as comfortable as a proper bed, but they both got to sleep well enough.

Mr Clarke looked back at them and welled up with parental pride. Rosie usually gave her brother a hard time but they'd pulled together now, just like they'd done when their mother died a year earlier. Paul even slept with his cheek resting on his big sister's shoulder.

Clarke himself was exhausted, but the roads were opening up as the refugees on foot made camp for the night and he didn't want to miss the chance to make progress. After driving further between ten and eleven o'clock than he'd managed in the previous four hours, he reached into the leather pocket inside his door, pulled out a small tin filled with Benzedrine pills and popped two into his mouth. The drug was a staple of salesmen, truck drivers and anyone else who couldn't afford to go to sleep.

*

At sunrise the Citroën formed part of a vast queue of vehicles waiting to cross a bridge into the town of Tours. Clarke was satisfied with his night's work, having driven more than a hundred kilometres beyond his original target of Orléans and making almost half of the distance between Paris and Bordeaux, where he hoped to find a ship to England.

But the car didn't budge for the next two hours. The kids woke up and while Paul dashed into the grass verge at the side of the road to urinate, Rosie played mother, dividing up stale bread, jam and left-over slices of a bacon joint for their breakfast.

'What's the hold-up?' Mr Clarke said, leaning out of the car and addressing a lanky man who was walking along the verge from the front of the queue.

'Looks like the army,' he explained. 'The Germans have bombed two of the bridges into town and the other one took a blast. There's a military convoy waiting to cross over, so the engineers are trying to shore it up.'

'Doesn't sound too good,' Mr Clarke said gravely. 'Is it possible to get over on foot?'

The man nodded, and rustled a paper bag containing two loaves of bread. 'People are walking across the railway bridge,' he explained. 'The centre of town isn't far. There are a few cafés open. I was dead lucky. I got to the bakery just as it opened; less than a dozen people in the queue.'

Mr Clarke thanked the man again and looked around at the kids in the back. 'Looks like we're going to be stuck here for a good while. How about we wander into town? We might be able to get some decent food and if the post office is open I might even have another stab at calling Henderson.'

'I thought he'd left the Embassy for good,' Paul said.

'I expect he has,' Mr Clarke said, nodding. 'But I've got his home number. There's a chance I'll catch him there.'

'What about the car?' Rosie asked. 'Is it safe to leave our things here? What if the Germans catch up with us?'

'We're still in French territory,' Mr Clarke said, as he got out and slammed his door. 'Our things should be safe for half an hour if we lock all the doors. The Germans didn't follow us out of Paris and their chances of finding us with so many people on the road are slim to nil.'

It was a glorious morning and although Tours had been bombed, the damage was light compared with the cities further north. What's more, it had been some time since the last air raid and there was a noticeable absence of smoke or the smell of burning.

For a few hundred metres Paul could almost imagine that the trip was part of a holiday outing. The illusion was shattered when they left the road and began clambering up a gravel embankment leading towards the railway tracks.

An old lady with horrible leg ulcers had made it up with two heavy bags, but the strain had done her in and she'd keeled over when she reached the top. She lay on her back, convulsing, while her tearful husband held her hand and dabbed her forehead with a handkerchief.

Like everyone else, Clarke and his children avoided eye contact as they walked by. Small acts of kindness were possible – helping to repair a broken cart, or carrying a crying child for a few kilometres – but nobody had the resources to deal with major crises and the only way to cope with the suffering was by shutting it out.

Once the Clarkes were across the bridge, a short scramble down a railway embankment and a gap in a wire fence took them into the commercial district on the south side of town.

'Used to be a big electrical store along there,' Mr Clarke said, aiming his pointing finger down a side street. 'The old girl who ran it would only deal with French or American companies. I could never sell the old buzzard a damned thing.'

Paul and Rosie both smiled as they brushed past

displaced people. The locals and refugees who'd travelled by car were hard to tell apart, but the ones who'd come on foot were stooped, dusty figures that lingered in every courtyard and doorway like a plague.

Mr Clarke was familiar with the street, but not exactly sure where it fitted into the overall layout of Tours. 'If I recall correctly there's a large square with a post office in that direction,' he said. But then he stepped into the empty road and shook his head. 'No, actually it's this way. *Definitely*.'

'You said that two streets ago,' Paul said.

As they walked down a pedestrian alleyway they passed by a tiny café, with just four tables and a line of stools in front of the counter. Mr Clarke caught the smell of coffee as Paul's eyes were drawn towards fresh baked croissants, piled on the countertop. They'd already passed a couple of cafés, but because of its obscure location this was the first that wasn't either closed or swamped with customers.

Paul and Rosie grabbed the only free table while their father walked to the counter to place their order. It came to three times what he'd expected to pay, but the proprietress shrugged and told him that coffee, flour and sugar were in short supply. Prices had skyrocketed and she was barely covering her costs.

As Mr Clarke settled at the table with his cup, he

heard a vague thumping sound and his coffee cup rattled against its saucer.

'Did you hear that?' Paul asked.

His question was answered by the whine of an air-raid siren. Everyone in the café sat up a little straighter as the proprietress stepped out from behind the counter and hurried to lock the café door.

'We get swarms of refugees in here otherwise,' she explained, to nobody in particular. 'If it gets bad, some of us can shelter under the stairs.'

As she stepped back towards the counter three young boys raced down the alleyway outside, followed by an enormously fat woman, straining the life out of a moped. Rosie found this sight hilarious and gave Paul a jab to make him turn and look.

'You wouldn't want her to sit on you,' he said, before laughing so hard that he blew the foam off his steamed milk.

Mr Clarke thought it was funny himself, but everyone in the tiny café could overhear so he reprimanded the kids for being rude. Before they could reply another explosion threw him forwards and coffee spilled over into his lap.

'Getting closer,' Rosie said, as she grabbed a napkin and threw it across the table at her dad.

Paul cocked his ear towards the window. The gloomy

alleyway muffled the sounds from above but aeroplane engines were now clearly audible. 'Sounds like there's a few of them,' he noted warily.

The third explosion was the loudest yet and it caused the giant espresso machine to lurch dangerously across the countertop. One of the valves broke open and pressurised steam began blasting out with a high-pitched whistle. The proprietress wrapped a cloth over her hand and tried turning a knob to stop it, but only succeeded in burning herself.

Her yelp brought an elderly man out from the back of the café. 'What happened?' he asked.

As he said this a bomb hit a building less than thirty metres away. Paul, Rosie and their father lurched one way before being thrown back the other. The large Venetian blind in the window clattered to the ground as a massive chunk of plaster dropped out of the ceiling.

Paul screamed out as it hit the woman at the next table with such force that her chair split and her face banged sickeningly against the tabletop. Out in the alleyway a great tearing sound erupted, followed by a storm of roof tiles and masonry. The electric lights flickered before going out and the metal tray of croissants clattered off the countertop as dust filled the air.

Mr Clarke caught a scent in his nostrils and immediately stood up. 'Gas leak,' he shouted, as he moved quickly towards the miraculously unbroken front window and looked up to check that the rubble had stopped raining down outside.

The others in the café could also smell gas and a man stubbed out his cigarette as Clarke frantically tugged at the door. The blast had made the building shift, causing the wooden door-frame to move and wedging the door itself firmly into position.

'Come on, you two,' he shouted to the kids, almost falling backwards as he got the door open.

As Paul, Rosie and everyone except the woman who'd been hit by the plaster piled out of the café, another bomb exploded. This one was several streets away, but the tremor was still enough to dislodge more roof tiles.

Paul looked up and saw a huge section of brickwork crashing towards him.

CHAPTER TWELVE

For the first time he could remember, Marc wasn't woken by the director yelling or other kids jumping on his bed. He was on a sofa, covered with a blanket. It took a few moments to remember how he'd got here and be hit with the immensity of what he'd done the night before.

He sat up, aching all over from the beating, as he looked at the dressing on his knee. Sabine, the waitress, had fixed it using bandage and cotton wool and whilst it looked rather dramatic it was clearly the work of someone who had no clue what they were doing.

Marc remembered how beautiful Sabine's painted nails were and her bright, lipsticked smile when she gave him the tissue to wipe his eyes. He pulled his legs off the sofa, put his foot down on something soft and shiny and realised to his horror that it was a bra.

He flicked it away with his big toe as he looked across the little bed-sit room and saw that Sabine wasn't in her bed. But her belongings were scattered everywhere: a dressing gown thrown down, a newspaper covered with bright red toenail clippings, a rug dusted with talcum powder.

Whichever way you cut it, Sabine was a slob. Marc stood up and looked around to make sure that his boots, clothes and money were present, then stepped warily across the wooden floor, both intrigued and horrified by Sabine's dirty underwear.

'Morning, skipper,' Sabine said, making Marc jump as she slid back the door of her tiny bathroom.

She wore only a lacy red bra and knickers and Marc was overpowered by a shot of lust, mangled with embarrassment. The only youngish women he knew were the nuns at the orphanage and even if one of them had ever appeared without her habit, he very much doubted that they wore underwear like *that*.

'Would you like your gown?' Marc spluttered as he pulled it off the floor, toppling a half-filled mug of mildewing coffee and cigarette ash.

'Aren't you a gentleman,' she said, as Marc rescued the cup.

When Sabine stepped up close to grab the gown her breasts were dead level with Marc's face. He didn't know where to look and he was so red he felt like his head was going to melt.

'You're the first person ever to call me a gentleman,' Marc said.

'And you're the first man who's ever encouraged me to put clothes on,' Sabine laughed. 'How's your knee?'

'OK, I think,' he said, grinning with relief as she covered up with the gown. 'You did a nice job with the bandage.'

'You think?' she said. 'I've never done one before. We can go downstairs and get some breakfast from the bar in a minute. Then I'll try sorting you out some transport so that you can get to your . . . who was it you said?'

'My uncle,' Marc lied. 'I need to get to Paris to see my uncle. Maybe I can go back to the station and see if there's a train.'

Marc cringed again as Sabine sat on the edge of her single bed and pulled a stocking up her leg.

'You won't need a train,' she said, shaking her head. 'There's always soldiers and truck drivers coming through the bar. I'll tell them you're my little nephew and get one of them to give you a lift.'

'I've got money,' Marc said.

'Oh don't worry about that.' Sabine smiled. 'A free beer and a flash of cleavage and they'll take you to Outer Mongolia if I ask them.'

'You think?' Marc smiled, but he didn't doubt it for a second. He was only too aware of how girls as pretty as Sabine can play tricks with your mind.

It was nine a.m. and downstairs the café was already open and doing a reasonable trade. Sabine was off duty, so she sat at a table with Marc and they ate croissants with jam. Once they'd eaten she eyed up a couple of rowdy military police officers out on the terrace and pushed her boobs out as she gave them a sob story about how her little nephew needed to get to Paris to see his parents and couldn't get on a train.

After dashing back upstairs to grab his things and kissing Sabine goodbye, Marc clambered into the filthy rear compartment of a canvas-covered army truck and set off towards Paris. He shared the space with a jangling mass of abandoned helmets and rifles, a crate of rattling cider bottles and two muddy Alsatians that looked ferocious, but seemed content to lie down and let the journey pass with as little fuss as possible.

Up front, the driver took great pleasure in blasting his horn and forcing refugees out of the road. It was cruel, but Marc couldn't help laughing as the passenger leaned out of the cab and yelled *ten points* for an elderly woman who fell over and *twenty-five* for a heavily laden handcart that toppled into a ditch.

'Peasants,' the driver said to Marc, when he pulled up and stood urinating over the back wheel of the truck. His posh accent indicated a good background. 'France is shit, the war is shit, everything's shit!'

'Vive la shitty France,' his companion yelled from up front.

Then the driver asked Marc to pass out four bottles of cider and told him that he could take one for himself. Marc had tasted alcohol a couple of times, but he'd never been drunk and didn't think it would be a good state in which to arrive in a strange city.

After climbing back into the cab, the driver set off even more erratically, swerving between lanes and blasting the horn. The speed also crept up and Marc could no longer see the funny side as he was thrown around the rear compartment. Even the dogs stood up and started scratching against the floor and barking like mad.

'Slow down!' Marc screamed, as he banged on the rear of the cab. 'You're gonna get us all killed.'

The passenger looked back through the little window. Cider drizzled from the corner of his mouth as he smiled at Marc. 'What's your problem?' he shouted. 'What do you think the Boche are gonna do when they get hold of us, eh? Don't you get it, kid? We're already as good as dead.'

At the next turn the tyres on one side lifted off the ground and crashed down, jarring Marc's back and shattering several of the remaining cider bottles. He couldn't see much of the road ahead through the small window into the cab, but he desperately grabbed one of the poles holding up the canvas roof as he sensed that they were braking hard. After a brief skid they were off-road, juddering violently as stones and rocks clattered against the truck's metal underside.

They came to a mercifully gentle halt as the truck fought a losing battle with heavy undergrowth. Marc was trembling and gasping for breath, but seemed free of serious injury. He thought it unlikely that the driver would be in any state to drive on but he wasn't prepared to take chances and, as the dogs scrambled back to their feet, he grabbed his bag and jumped out the back.

He landed in a tangle of earth and roots torn up by the truck. Thirty metres away the road was lined with the bedraggled column of open-backed troop carriers and horse-drawn artillery that the driver had swerved to avoid.

An officer with his pistol drawn was jogging towards Marc with three of his men a few paces behind. A second group was cutting through the trees towards the front of the truck.

'Hands up,' the officer shouted to Marc. 'What the devil is this?'

Marc didn't like having a gun pointed at him. 'I was just riding in the back,' he explained nervously. 'They went crazy.'

As the team at the front of the truck grabbed the doors and pulled out the driver and his companion, one of the bewildered Alsatians scrambled over the back flap and yelped pitifully.

'Big branch straight through the windscreen, sir,' one of the soldiers at the front shouted. 'Driver's dead for sure and the other bloke's in a right mess.'

The officer turned away and shook his head. 'Drunks,' he sneered. 'Deserters, most likely, and I'm not wasting any more time on them. Let's move out.'

'Are you heading to Paris?' Marc asked. 'Can I get a ride?'

The officer looked as though his head was going to explode. 'Piss off, *boy*. This is the French Army, not a bloody taxi service.'

But one of the soldiers was more sympathetic. 'You're only a few kilometres out and our horses are tired. You'll do just as well to walk.'

'What about the dogs, sir? Shall we bring them along?' his colleague asked.

'What the bloody hell do I want with a couple of filthy

dogs?' the officer shouted. 'Shoot them. Might as well put the other bugger out of his misery too if you don't think he's going to make it.'

The soldier alongside the officer pulled up his rifle and shot the Alsatian clean through the head. It was harder to see the second dog inside the truck and the first shot hit it in the gut. It squealed desperately for several seconds before a second blast put it out of its misery.

Marc waited to hear a fourth shot as he staggered back towards the road, shaking with fear. But despite the officer's suggestion to put the man out of his misery, the bullet never came.

CHAPTER THIRTEEN

Paul backed up to the side of an apartment block and wrapped his arms over his head as masonry crashed around him. The giant slab of bricks hit the opposite wall of the narrow alleyway and took on a spin before crashing down less than two metres from where he cowered. Pebble-sized chunks pelted his body as the mortar shattered.

'Dad?' Paul shouted.

He opened his eyes a fraction, only for them to be forced shut by the dust swirling through the air. The worst of the collapse had passed, but single bricks still chinked down and a woman screamed horribly. At least it wasn't Rosie.

A second later, Paul felt a tug on his arm. Half

blind and his mouth filled with dust, Mr Clarke dragged his son towards the early sunlight piercing the end of the alleyway.

'Did you see Rosie?' Mr Clarke asked.

Paul was coughing violently and couldn't answer.

'Rosie?' Mr Clarke bellowed.

She'd sprinted ahead and stood at the end of the alleyway, in better shape than her male relatives. The German planes continued to drone as Paul forced himself to open his eyes and blink out the grit. They'd emerged into a busy square filled with dust, flames and panic. When Paul got some focus he saw the wreckage of market stalls. Every building had shattered windows and a horse thrashed helplessly on its side. Its hind quarters were badly burned and it was pinned down by the charred remains of a cart harnessed to its back.

Rosie looked anxiously at her brother's torn and blood-spattered shirt sleeve. 'Show me your hand.'

Paul raised his arm and saw that it was peppered with scratches and cuts. He'd hardly noticed because his grit-filled eyes were much more painful.

'We'll have to find some water and get that cleaned up,' Rosie said. 'Your head's cut too.'

Paul was aware of a stinging sensation just above his ear and he felt with his fingertips until he found some hair matted with blood.

'Oh, that's clever,' Rosie said. 'Stick your filthy fingers in and get it infected.'

'What can we do now?' Paul asked, ignoring his sister and looking up at his dad.

But Mr Clarke was in a daze.

A terrible moan went up as a man hoisted an elderly woman on to his back. Her face and torso had been shredded by flying glass. Another man was calling out for a gun to put the burned horse out of its misery.

'You've got a gun,' Rosie said, giving her father a nudge.

'Don't be bloody daft,' Mr Clarke said irritably. 'I'm a foreigner walking around with a German pistol. Do you want me to get arrested?'

Rosie backed off and shook her hands furiously. 'Well don't just stand there, Dad! What *do* you want us to do?'

'OK . . .' Mr Clarke mumbled. 'I'm trying to think . . . Can you remember the way back to the car?'

'The alleyway's blocked off with rubble,' Paul noted.

But Rosie nodded. 'I'm sure I can find another way back towards the river.'

'Good,' Clarke said, pointing across the square towards a post office. 'You take Paul back to the car and use my first aid kit to clean up his cuts. I'm going over there to see if I can get a call through to Henderson in Paris and maybe pick up some bread if the queues aren't too bad.'

Mr Clarke got out his wallet and gave his daughter a ten-franc note. 'In case you come across a place selling bread, or some other kind of food that you fancy.'

'What if we end up buying the same thing?' Rosie asked.

Mr Clarke shrugged. 'With the Germans smashing up the roads and bridges, supplies are going to get short. I'd rather we end up with too much food than not enough. Now start heading back and I'll meet you back at the car in twenty minutes or so.'

'Maybe we should stick together,' Paul said. 'My arm doesn't hurt much.'

As Paul was speaking his sister realised that the aircraft had dropped out of sight, whilst the sound of their engines was getting louder. This could only mean that the pilots were coming in over the rooftops for a machine-gun attack. People in the square started running for cover and a few screams went up as a fighter cleared the flag post on top of a small civic building and let rip.

Travelling at two hundred kilometres an hour, the line of bullets crossed the square in under three seconds. Most pulsed off the cobbles and ricocheted widely, retaining enough force to kill. Direct hits pounded market stalls, tore up cars and occasionally hit human flesh.

Paul's heart slammed as he dived into a doorway between two shop fronts with his father and Rosie bundled on top of him. He looked up, but his father forced his head down.

'There's more coming,' Clarke explained.

Over the next half minute three more fighters skimmed low over the square, firing their machine guns and causing a wave of screams. There were more injured and some dead, but at least the horse got finished off.

After the fighters came a taut, dusty silence. Paul looked up and saw a fresh bullet hole in the masonry less than thirty centimetres above them.

'Too close,' Rosie gasped, close to tears and with her hands shaking.

A few metres ahead, a boy of about six cowered under the rusted frame of a market stall.

'This square is too open,' Mr Clarke said. 'It's a shooting gallery. Keep to the side streets as you walk back to the car.'

Another blast of machine-gun fire ripped off in the distance and an elderly refugee with his coat over his head kept rocking back and forth yelling, '*I can't stand it,*' over and over.

'There's a dot of blood on your shirt, Dad,' Rosie noted.

Mr Clarke looked down and saw a coin-sized circle of blood just below his nipple. 'Shrapnel,' he explained. 'Just a nick.'

High above them, an aeroplane was going into a dive.

'Stuka,' Mr Clarke yelled, as he grabbed Rosie's hand.

The risk of falling masonry in a bomb blast made Clarke avoid the narrow alleyway they'd emerged from minutes earlier. He led his kids across the cobbles and made it into a side street as the first of three bombs exploded. The first two hit the marketplace, slaughtering many who'd already been shot, along with those struggling to drag them out of harm's way. The third bomb hit the front steps of the civic hall, demolishing the front porch and tearing a hole in the façade that exposed desks and filing cabinets on the upper floors.

The Clarkes moved briskly into the side street, chased by dust and the sickly smell of burned meat. Rosie realised it was human flesh, but knew she had to keep the thought out of her head if she wanted to avoid breaking down.

'What about the little boy under the table?' Paul asked anxiously. 'Did either of you see him after—'

Before Paul could finish his father stopped moving, to the consternation of a woman running behind with a pram who had to swerve out of his way. Mr Clarke had grabbed his handkerchief and began coughing into it.

'Are you OK?' Paul asked.

'It's the dust,' Rosie said, shielding her eyes with a hand.

But as Clarke pulled the handkerchief away from his face, he spattered his daughter with blood.

'Oh god,' Rosie gasped. 'Dad!'

With each cough Clarke wheezed desperately for air but his throat was clogged with blood, and the coin-sized patch on his shirt had turned into a soggy red dinner-plate.

'What's happening?' Paul asked, as Rosie grabbed her father's arm and helped him to sit on the kerb.

'Deeper,' Mr Clarke croaked, as he looked desperately at the wound in his chest. 'Must be . . .'

'It's right where his heart is, or his lung . . . or something,' Rosie said, glancing around desperately. As legs swept by she realised that theirs was just one crisis amidst a hundred.

'Henderson,' he croaked, as the blood-soaked handkerchief fell away from his face. 'Find him. Give him the papers.'

'You're not going to die, Dad,' Paul said, more out of hope than conviction.

Mr Clarke used the last of his energy to look at his son and mouth the word *Sorry* with his bloody lips.

'Dad!' Rosie screamed, shaking him as she glanced all around. 'Just hang on, there must be someone . . .'

But suddenly there was no resistance and Mr Clarke's head flopped backwards. Unmoving eyes stared at her, glazed and still, like a pair of marbles.

CHAPTER FOURTEEN

It's hard to grasp when something so big happens. Paul and Rosie felt like some giant magnet held them in place. They kept looking at each other, then back at their father, to confirm that he was really dead.

Several minutes passed. The dust from the explosions settled and the aeroplanes retreated into the surrounding countryside, but neither Paul nor Rosie spoke. Their first sentence had to capture the enormity of what had happened and they couldn't find the words.

Normally there would be a safety net – police, ambulance, telephones – but they'd seen enough of the evacuation to know that normal rules didn't apply. They'd stepped over death and looked away from pain and now it was their turn to be the ones sitting at the roadside while the world passed by.

'I've lost my mummy,' a small boy said.

It was the lad Paul had seen hiding under the market stall. He was stocky, no more than six, and so dusty that he could have been a statue of himself. Part of Rosie wanted to tell him to scram because she had enough problems, but he was a cute little thing and it was a relief to have something else to focus on.

'Where did you last see her?' Rosie asked gently. 'Maybe she ran to the other side of the square.'

'I don't know,' the boy said, after which their faces took up the conversation. The boy's eyes asked if it was OK to sit down beside them on the kerb and Rosie's nod indicated that it was.

'I'm Hugo,' the boy said.

'Are you from Tours?'

'Hugo Charmain. Seventh arrondissement[3], Paris,' the boy said grandly. As he spoke he pulled a piece of string out from inside his shirt. A label with his name and address was attached to the end.

'Were you just with your mummy?' Paul asked.

Hugo nodded sadly, before looking at Mr Clarke. 'My daddy is fighting for France. Is that yours?'

---

[3] Seventh arrondissement – a district of Paris, similar to a British postal district.

'Yes,' Rosie said.

'Why did he die?' Hugo asked, but neither Paul nor Rosie gave an answer.

The entrance to the bombed square was less than thirty metres away. A number of small fires had turned into one inferno now and refugees were wading into the smoke to gather handcarts and suitcases abandoned in the rubble.

Paul looked gravely at his sister. 'What can we do now?'

'I . . .' Rosie said, before pausing to think. 'We have to stay calm. We'll have to leave Dad here, but take his money and all of his valuables so that they're not stolen. Then we'll go back to the car and get the documents.'

'Have you ever driven the car?' Paul asked. 'Do you think we could?'

Rosie shook her head. 'I've watched Dad, but I've never worked it out.'

'So how do we get south?' Paul asked anxiously.

'We'll have to improvise. Maybe we can walk. It might take days, though, and those documents weigh a tonne. Or maybe we could find another refugee who can drive but doesn't have a car. Then they can drive us.'

'That might work,' Paul agreed. 'But we should try calling Henderson first.'

Rosie nodded. 'Although Dad couldn't track him

down yesterday, and I'm not even sure if his number is written down anywhere.'

'Maybe if we stay here, Henderson will come and find us.'

Rosie tutted. 'Don't be thick, Paul. There's about a million people on the road. How's he going to do that?'

'I don't know. I could draw a big sign or something.'

Rosie shook her head with contempt. 'He doesn't even know that Dad's dead. We're on our own.'

'All right,' Paul said irritably. 'I'm just thinking out loud.'

'Besides, whatever we do we've got to be discreet,' Rosie continued. 'The German agents could be out looking for us too.'

The string of events was so overpowering that Paul had forgotten that it began with a German agent in his bedroom less than twenty-four hours earlier. 'What if the police are looking for us too?' he asked.

'They'll have found the dead bodies in our apartment,' Rosie said, nodding. 'There's bound to be an investigation, but hopefully they've got other things on their minds right now.'

'I'm going to look for my mummy,' Hugo said, as he stood up and raced off towards the square.

There was an innocence about Hugo's words that choked Rosie up. He made it sound like he was going into the garden to kick a ball around. How would the little boy react if he found his mummy badly burned or injured? Rosie wanted to help, but she was engulfed in her own problems and within a few seconds Hugo had vanished into the smoke.

Rosie began undoing her father's jacket. She took out his pocket book and wallet. 'Get his watch and his rings, Paul.'

Paul had never touched a dead person before. He wanted to argue with Rosie, because taking a wallet from a jacket seemed far less ghoulish than prising off rings.

'Maybe we should leave him be,' Paul said. 'Out of respect.'

This annoyed Rosie and her natural bossiness surfaced. 'I don't know about you, Paul, but I haven't got a cheque book or a bank account. A ring or a watch might buy us food or petrol on the road.'

'OK,' Paul said. 'Don't bite my head off.'

But he didn't mind being angry with his sister. It gave him something to focus on while twisting the rings off his dead father's hand. It took less than a minute for the pair to strip away everything of value.

Rosie stood up and handed Paul the gun. But she was older and bossier, and it seemed all wrong.

'What do you want me to do with that?' he asked, shaking his head fretfully.

'Tuck it in your trousers,' Rosie explained. 'I'm wearing a summer dress. What am I gonna do, stick it up my bum?'

Paul pushed the gun down his trousers and pulled his shirt out to cover it over.

'Let's move,' Rosie said coldly.

'What about Dad's body?'

'Stick around feeling sorry if you want. But I don't plan on being here when the planes come back.'

Paul was indignant. 'How come you're so heartless?'

'I'm *not* heartless,' Rosie snapped, as she grabbed Paul by the scruff of his shirt and yanked him in close. 'Do you think I'm happy about this? Do you think I don't feel like sitting on the kerb crying my eyes out? But the bombs dropping out of the sky are *real*, Paul. The German armies heading towards us are *real*. We've got to be strong because weak people are dying all around and nobody gives a damn.'

A tear streaked down Rosie's cheek as she shoved her startled brother away.

'Now you've made me cry,' Rosie said aggressively, as she bent forwards and kissed her father's forehead. 'I can't look at him any more.'

After the kiss, Rosie began to walk away. Paul hurriedly removed his father's bloody cravat. Then he straightened the silk square by flicking it in the air and laid it over his father's face. The wind would probably blow it away, but it was the only dignified gesture he could think of.

Paul felt weird as he realised he'd never see the face beneath the cravat again. For a moment he felt like he was going to shit his pants, but he managed to stand up and dash after his sister.

'Rosie . . . *Rosie!* Wait!'

*

It's hard to think if you're moving fast and Rosie didn't want to think about anything. Smaller and weaker, Paul struggled to keep up but knew that he had to because Rosie was all he had left. The army had shored up the damaged bridge and although they'd been away from the car for less than half an hour the great queue of traffic that had driven swiftly through the night had moved on and been replaced by a thinly spaced convoy of horses, handcarts and dirty humans.

'Where's it gone?' Paul shouted, as he approached a distinctive kink in the road where he was sure they'd left the car.

Rosie was twenty metres ahead and she'd already eyed the outline of the Citroën through a pair of trees. The vehicle leaned forwards with its front wheels tilted into a ditch. She gasped as she scrambled towards it. The back end had a long dent where a high vehicle – most likely a truck – had forced it off the road.

'Is it OK?' Paul asked breathlessly as he raced up behind his sister. 'How are we gonna pull it out of there?'

As Rosie walked around to the passenger side, she could smell petrol and noticed a dark patch on the earth, with the screw-in filler cap lying beside it.

'They've siphoned off our petrol,' Rosie gasped. 'There goes our chance of getting someone to drive us.'

'Damn,' Paul said, slapping his hands against his thighs, before looking inside the car. 'It doesn't look like anything's been touched inside.'

Rosie unlocked the trunk and sure enough their luggage remained.

'Maybe we could buy some petrol in town,' Paul suggested, as he opened the back door and leaned in. The smell of cracked leather and his father's hair tonic now seemed like part of some other kid's life.

'No chance,' Rosie said. 'I haven't seen a petrol pump without a sold-out sign on it since we left Paris.'

'What about Dad's watch? It's gold, it must be worth way more than a tank of petrol.'

Rosie shrugged forlornly. 'Paul, right now I doubt we'd be able to buy a tank of petrol if the entire trunk was filled with thousand-franc notes. Besides, I doubt his watch is worth much. Dad had a decent job and we're better off than most, but we're not millionaires you know.'

When he was little Paul had often been rebuked for messing around with his father's watch and this had given him an exalted sense of its value. Now he realised it was nothing more than battered gold plate.

'So what *are* we supposed to do then?'

She shrugged again. 'We can't stick around here, and it's only a matter of time before someone robs the car.'

'Dad loved this car,' Paul said sadly.

'Well, we can't carry it on our backs, can we? He would have had to abandon it or sell it for next to nothing when we got to Bordeaux anyway.'

'I suppose.' Paul nodded.

'We'll just have to gather up as much as we can carry. Mum's jewellery, a few bits of clothing and the documents. Then we'll head back into town and try contacting Henderson by telephone. If that doesn't work we'll have to move south on foot. We're both healthy – we should be able to walk it in four or five days.'

'I guess,' Paul said warily. 'I just hope the German tanks don't beat us to it.'

CHAPTER FIFTEEN

Marc felt like he was going to wake up. It would be one of those intense dreams, where your back is all sweaty and it takes a couple of seconds to realise that it's not for real. But Paris *was* real.

For an hour he walked through streets of apartment blocks. Sometimes along grand boulevards with more cars queuing at the traffic lights than he saw passing the orphanage in a week. Other roads were narrow, with crates of bottles, overflowing bins and the smell of piss in the air.

These outer streets went on for so long that Marc began to wonder if he was going in circles. But occasional glimpses of the city centre reassured him, with the tall buildings gradually growing in size. He passed several

Metro stations that could have whisked him away, but he'd never been on a train before and somehow imagined that he'd make a fool of himself or, worse, get mangled on an escalator or trapped between the doors.

There were signs of war everywhere: sandbags piled up in front of windows, anti-aircraft guns in the squares and German planes skimming overhead. The previous night had seen the heaviest bombardment of the war and Paris was capped by a cloud of ash and smoke that kept the sun under wraps. But the scale of the city made the odds of actually being shot or bombed seem slight.

Marc had spent his whole life dreaming about running away to Paris, but the longer he walked the more reality wore him down. He'd managed a good breakfast, but soon he'd be hungry again. Soon he'd need lunch, and dinner and a place to sleep, and clean clothes and . . . Human needs are relentless. The money would run out. He'd have to find work, or steal, or . . .

But he'd known that from the start and he reckoned he'd done OK so far. Marc realised, as he approached it, that the city centre would bring no great revelation and would probably be more crowded and intimidating than the outlying districts. He decided to make a go of finding some food and a place to stay in the next decent neighbourhood he came to.

It happened to be a small shopping street two

kilometres north of the city centre. One of hundreds throughout the city where locals bought food, newspapers, had their clothes laundered and gossiped in a café.

Marc stopped by the grand frontage of a cinema with posters for an American movie *in colour*. But it was early, and the metal grilles were pulled down over the front. At the orphanage the nuns would rig up a projector and let the boys watch silent comedies every Christmas, but Marc had never been to a proper cinema and the prospect excited him. At the side of the cinema was a sizeable but largely empty café. After a second's hesitation he stepped inside. The miserable-looking waitress took one glance and decided that she didn't like him.

'Refugee?' she snorted.

Marc nodded. There was no point denying it – he was filthy after getting bounced around inside the army truck and any children still living in Paris would be at school.

'Do you have money?' she asked, blocking Marc's path before he could get near a table.

He pulled a small bundle of notes from a trouser pocket – Sabine had advised him to divide the money between his pigskin bag and several pockets so that he couldn't lose all of it at once.

The woman crinkled her nose and dragged a chair

out from a table. 'It's too early for lunch, but I can fix you a plate.'

Marc nodded. 'Would you mind filling my bottle of water?'

The waitress looked like this was a great imposition, but eventually snatched the empty bottle. The only other customers sat three tables across. Much to Marc's relief the miserable waitress sat herself at a distant table and lit a cigarette. His food and refilled water bottle were brought out by a great barrel of a man. It comprised a bowl of soup with stringy meat in it, along with chunks of bread and slices of cheese.

'Whereabouts are you from?' the man asked, as he ran his fat hand through a beard.

Marc felt uneasy. The only men he'd ever dealt with were Director Tomas and a pair of schoolmasters who rivalled him in ferocity. 'Near Beauvais, sir,' he said politely, as he dipped a spoon into his soup. Then he shuddered and wondered if he should have told a lie.

'Beauvais, eh?' the man said, clearly intrigued. 'How long ago? What's the situation up there?'

'I left early this morning. There are quite a lot of planes, regular bombing and stuff.'

'Artillery?' the man asked. 'Sorry to be a pest, but the news on Radio France isn't worth a damn.'

Marc couldn't help smiling at the swear-word, and his

tension eased as he realised the man just wanted to know when he could expect Germans on his doorstep. 'I didn't see any shelling myself, but I heard that there was some.'

The man nodded solemnly. 'Artillery would put the Boche within twenty kilometres. Did you see troops retreating?'

'A few,' Marc said.

'I'd say they'll reach Paris within five days, a week at most.'

'Will you leave?'

'At the drop of a hat,' the man said, smiling, but then he pointed a thumb at the miserable waitress. 'But my wife says no.'

The waitress looked up from her magazine and yelled across the café. 'I'd rather be shelled by the Boche than live with your relatives.'

'Word of advice, my boy,' the man whispered, as he theatrically shielded his mouth with his hand. 'Don't *ever* get married.'

Marc smiled. He felt a lot more comfortable than when he'd entered and decided to ask a question. 'Is there anywhere around here I could stay?'

The man raised an eyebrow. 'I thought you'd be heading south.'

'Probably.' Marc shrugged.

'But you're all alone. Aren't you meeting up with someone?'

'Yes,' Marc lied hurriedly. 'I've got an uncle down south. But it's safer to walk by night. Easier to take cover.'

'Ahh.' The man nodded. 'Sensible. You might find a bed at the Dormitory Raquel. It's a rough old place though: labourers, kitchen staff. Mostly Russians and Poles. But it's cheap and I doubt they'd mind taking a boy if you pay up front.'

Marc didn't seem sure. 'So you'd recommend it?'

The man broke into a booming laugh. 'I'd recommend the Ritz. But judging by the state of your clothing your budget won't stretch to five thousand francs a night.'

'You're right there,' Marc smiled, as he mopped up the last of his soup with the bread.

After Marc had handed over payment, the man tore a sheet off the notepad inside his apron and sketched out the route to the Dormitory Raquel.

'Thanks very much,' Marc said, as he quickly checked the map to ensure it made sense. 'So I turn left out of here?'

The man nodded. Marc didn't catch exactly what his wife said as he walked out, but the tone was definitely caustic.

As Marc followed the pencil markings on the map – second left by the big church – he felt a little more settled but also bloated, because he'd eaten two meals and it wasn't yet noon. After the church he began walking up a steep hill along a street of detached houses.

They had once been luxurious residences, but the neighbourhood had clearly fallen out of fashion. Façades were cracked, windows boarded and front gardens were pocket-sized jungles. To make matters even more depressing, the sky seemed to be darkening for a storm.

The last house in the street was Dormitory Raquel. Marc stepped up a front path with moss growing through cracks in the concrete and nervously approached the front door, on which hung a great list of rules: *No credit, no pets, no Jews, no Senegalese, no gambling, no noise, no women, no singing, no smoking in bed and absolutely no refunds.* Beneath this, the list was repeated in other languages for the benefit of Poles, Russians and Germans.

'Hello?' Marc said nervously as he pushed the front door open.

He jumped as a toilet cistern thundered in a small room to his left. The door opened and a bare-chested man emerged, followed by an appalling stench that didn't mix well with Marc's full stomach. He briefly glimpsed into the room and saw mould on the walls, a rusted cistern and a toilet that looked as if it hadn't been cleaned in decades.

'Sorry,' the man said, speaking bad French with a

Russian accent. 'Didn't know you were waiting.'

Marc cleared his throat. 'Do you work here? I was thinking about getting a bed.'

The man pointed at the ceiling. 'Madame Raquel, she's upstairs.'

As Marc moved deeper into the house, he was overwhelmed by the smell of cigarettes and old sweat. By the time he reached the top of the stairs he wanted to turn away and run out, but he was stunned as he looked into a dormitory and saw an elderly man lying naked on his bed. He had a wild beard in which chunks of his own vomit hung like Christmas decorations.

There were four beds crammed into the room and the sheets on each were stained yellow and singed with dozens of cigarette burns. The window was boarded over and the filthy linoleum floor was strewn with beer bottles and newspaper.

Marc was horrified; he hadn't come to Paris to end up living in such squalor. At least at the orphanage the nuns made all the boys bathe and change clothes regularly. He was about to turn and run back down the stairs when a large woman that he took to be Madame Raquel emerged from a bedroom with a stern face.

'Any more bother from you,' she said, wagging her finger at a patron, 'any more, and I'll have my lads break every bone in your body and throw you out in the gutter where you belong.' Then she turned to Marc. 'Who are you looking for, kid?'

'Erm, how much is a bed?' he asked meekly.

'Six francs a night up here. Eight downstairs, which includes breakfast. Minimum stay is three nights and a ten-franc deposit on your sheets. Any messing around and you're out on your arse. No refunds.'

Marc nodded uncertainly.

After a few moments' silence, Madame Raquel lost her cool. 'So?' she shouted. 'Haven't got all day. Do you want a bed or not?'

Marc shuddered with fright. Raquel scared him and he felt his hand drifting obediently towards the money in his trousers, but then he heard steps behind him and he saw that the old man now stood naked in the doorway of his bedroom.

'Put some clothes on, you dirty old bastard,' Raquel shouted.

Marc knew there was no way he could stay here, but he was too scared to say so in case Madame Raquel had a go at him.

'I don't have my money with me,' Marc said weakly. 'I'll come back later.'

He turned to hurry down the stairs, but the naked man was ahead of him and he was forced to watch as the old tramp staggered down to the toilet, while Madame

Raquel gave him a stare that made his face hot.

'You won't find anywhere cheaper,' she shouted, as Marc finally had a chance to run down the staircase. He stepped out on to the doorstep and inhaled fresh air as if his life depended upon it. He hadn't touched anything inside the house, but just being in there made his skin crawl and he'd sooner have spent a night in the cowshed on Morel's farm.

Marc started walking back down the hill. He was disappointed that he hadn't solved the accommodation problem and wondered about going back to the café and asking the friendly man if he knew of a slightly more upmarket dorm. But his paranoid side put him off: maybe the waiter knew how vile the Dormitory Raquel was and had sent him there as a joke.

The sky was now black, but Marc didn't mind the prospect of rain. The atmosphere was smoky from the bombing and he thought it would clear the air. By the time he was halfway down the hill a few spots had started hitting the pavement. They seemed unusually dark, but he wasn't alarmed until a drop ran down his forehead and touched his eyelid.

Suddenly his eye was stinging and, as the rain grew harder, he noticed that each drop hitting his shirt left a grey stain behind. The fires that had burned after the previous night's air raid had sent millions of tonnes of smoke and ash into the atmosphere and now it was falling as black rain.

A gust of wind turned the rain into a dark curtain. Marc had grey streaks running all over his skin as he closed his mouth tight and shielded his eyes with a hand. He glanced around desperately for somewhere to shelter. The church at the bottom of the hill would have been ideal, but it was still a couple of minutes away, even if he ran.

Marc noticed that the nearest house had a small porch. The front gate was blocked by the overgrown hedge on either side, but he ducked through and ran up to the front door, then stood under a stone archway just as the rain started to really belt down.

Dark swirls streamed down a path made from black and white tiles as Marc stared through a crack in the wooden shutters into the front room. Given the state of the garden he was surprised to see that it was reasonably well furnished, although he noticed that the soft furnishings were covered in brown dustsheets, as if the owner had gone away for a long time.

As the rain pelted, Marc started wondering about the house. It looked pretty comfortable inside and, with the Germans on the march, it didn't seem likely that the owner would be returning any time soon. Maybe he could break in.

CHAPTER SIXTEEN

Rosie cleaned up Paul's cuts with disinfectant, then they began sorting through the luggage and packing bare essentials into two small suitcases: clothes, their mother's jewellery, their father's gold cufflinks, a French road map, toothbrushes and a few small items of toiletries. The most painful decision was over the photo album. They'd never manage to carry the whole thing, with its heavy cardboard cover, so they each took a few favourites and solemnly left behind hundreds of photographs mounted on black pages, with comments written in white pencil by their mother.

Then the siblings made a careful study of their father's wallet and pocket book to see if they could find a number for Charles Henderson. They sat close on the dry grass beside the car, wading through scribbled notes and details of department-store buyers, shipping-line engineers, members of the French military and jottings on restaurants and hotels where their father had found a good meal or comfortable bed during his days on the road. But they couldn't find any contact details for Henderson.

'Hopeless,' Rosie declared, after three-quarters of an hour. 'I think we'd better get moving.'

Paul insisted on taking his best drawings and pens and as she was older and stronger, Rosie took both her belongings and the case with the documents inside. It was a dead weight and she was forced to switch arms even before they'd walked a full kilometre.

'We need a pram or a trolley,' Rosie said. 'Quite a few people died in the square – we might find one abandoned there.'

'I guess,' Paul said. 'But it probably would have been blasted to bits.'

'Well maybe there's a shop then,' Rosie said. 'You know, one that sells old prams or something? There's no way I can lug all this lot to Bordeaux.'

Paul looked uncertainly at his sister. 'If we go back to the square, do you think Dad might still be there?'

'How should I know?' Rosie snapped. 'If you've got better ideas, Paul, I'm all ears.'

A few local trains seemed to be running and a railwayman stood at the bottom of the bridge, ordering the stream of refugees not to cross. Instead, they had to walk more than two kilometres to the road bridge that had been repaired by the army and then another kilometre back to the centre of Tours.

By the time Paul and Rosie reached the town centre their shoulders ached and their clothes were darkened by sweat. Every so often a car would hoot all of the pedestrians out of the road, giving the pair a stark reminder of how their status had plummeted.

Still, they had their health, which was more than could be said for those who'd already spent days on their feet. They were also far from the only unaccompanied children on the road. In some instances mothers had been killed, leaving kids of Rosie's age in charge of younger siblings and carts laden with an entire family's possessions.

The bombed square had been sealed off with wooden barriers and the cobbles were awash with huge puddles where the fire service had successfully attacked multiple blazes. Only a few smouldering embers remained and these were under careful watch from firemen who doused them with spray from their hoses.

Paul could not help but glance towards the doorway where their father had died. It was now empty.

But the biggest change since they'd left the square was that the roof of the civic building had caught light and collapsed on to the floors below it. The resulting cascade had left a spectacular mound of rubble and burnt office furniture, with two scorched walls standing erect on either side.

'Useless,' Paul groaned, as he stared at the mangled carcasses of market stalls. 'There's no trolley here.'

'Excuse me,' Rosie said, as she approached an exhausted-looking fireman who stood in front of a red and white barrier, puffing on a cigarette. 'Do you know the town well?'

'Lived here all my life,' he said, nodding.

'We need a trolley or a pram,' Rosie explained. 'Any idea where we might get hold of one?'

The fireman looked unsure, but after a few seconds he made a gesture with his hand. 'Two streets over that way there's a road with a couple of second-hand shops. But right now there are certain things that can't be had for any amount of money and I suspect wheeled carts are one of them.'

Paul looked dejected as they turned away.

'There is one thing,' the fireman called after them, brightening up as he pointed in the opposite direction. 'You could try St Peter's church. The priest has been helping out refugees all week. It's a two-minute walk and if there's anyone who can help you, he's your man.'

'Thanks,' Rosie said, smiling. 'We'll give it a go.'

They dragged the cases for another hundred metres until they found a side street with a gothic church behind tall iron gates. It was approaching the middle of the day and with the sun high, the church's well-tended garden and neat surrounding lawns made an extraordinary oasis amidst the chaos of the bombed town. But as the siblings passed through the gates, they were shocked by a line of bodies. They had all been covered with sheets or clothing, but in many cases blood had soaked through and flies swarmed to the smell.

'It's you!' Hugo said excitedly, as he ran out of the church doorway, pointing at the largest of the bodies. 'There's your daddy. I told them about you, but I don't know your names.'

Paul was stunned by the reappearance of his dad, but the real horror was the two bodies of young children laid out alongside. None of the deaths was just, but the death of kids too small to even know what war was seemed like the worst thing of all.

'Did you find your mummy?' Rosie asked.

Hugo nodded, before pointing into the distance. 'They took her away. These are ones nobody knows.'

'Hello,' a priest said brightly, as he stepped into the sun from the church's main archway. He was tall, thin and had a huge growth on one side of his nose. 'I'm Father Leroy. Do you two need any assistance?'

'The boy and girl from the dead man!' Hugo explained excitedly, which was enough to stop the priest in his tracks.

'My children,' he said softly. 'Bless you. Come inside and we can talk.'

CHAPTER SEVENTEEN

As Marc stood under the porch waiting for the storm to pass, he recalled Director Tomas' many lectures on the places where hooligans like him could end up if they continued to misbehave. France had a brutal penal system that ran from rat-infested dungeons with twenty men crammed into each cell, to labour camps and penal colonies where twelve-hour shifts and starvation rations were the norm.

Marc had already stolen from the director and run away, but those crimes were within the bounds of the orphanage. Tomas would have been within his rights to call in the police, but he'd never do so because beating the daylights out of his charges gave him such pleasure.

But however horrible the orphanage could be, the

director was a devil Marc knew. If he was caught breaking into a house in Paris, he'd face punishment by police and the courts. He neither knew nor understood these forces, but the prospect of a Paris jail cell chilled his heart.

Against this, Marc weighed the extraordinary filth he'd seen inside Dormitory Raquel and the fact that sooner or later the director's savings would run out and he'd have no option but to break the law to survive. Everything in life costs and he was too young for an honest job.

If he didn't break into the house now it was only delaying the inevitable and the obvious absence of the owner, combined with the overgrown hedges shielding the view from the street, made this a great opportunity. The only thing was, Marc didn't have a clue how to break into a house.

When the sun finally broke between two banks of cloud, Marc stepped off the porch and began a circuit of the building. His white shirt was now grey from the falling ash and his eyes still stung, but the rain had scrubbed the air and Marc felt as if he was breathing properly for the first time since he'd left the countryside.

He had to battle shrubs and branches as he searched for an easy way in. Most of the shutters were closed, but where he could see inside he was reassured by rolled-up rugs and covers over all the furniture.

Marc hadn't found the soft entry point he'd hoped for, but the best option seemed to be a small window made from frosted glass slats. He wasn't tall enough to reach it easily, so he dragged a metal dustbin from the back of the house and stood on top.

It was easy to put his fingers between two slats and pull on them. There was a squeal as all six swivelled into a horizontal position, giving him a good view into a bathroom. Directly beneath the window was a washbasin, with a spider's web spanning the taps and the edge of the bowl. Across the room was a toilet, a bidet and a large bath standing on four tarnished feet. Like the house itself, the fixtures were grand but clearly a few decades past their prime.

If he could get two or three slats out, Marc thought he'd be able to slide through the window and drop down on to the sink. He began with an experimental pull on a slat, then he gave it a wiggle, but it clearly wasn't going to be that easy.

Marc studied the rusted metal frame into which each slat was mounted. The slats were joined to the frame by a screw at each end and although he didn't have a screwdriver, he reckoned he'd be able to loosen the screw at each end using the director's hunting knife and then pull them out.

He stumbled as he jumped down off the bin, but he

wasn't hurt and within half a minute he'd grabbed the hunting knife out of the pigskin bag and was trying to get the sharp edge of the blade into a screw head. However, the blade wasn't really the right width and even when he did manage to get the blade in line to apply some force, the screw didn't budge because it was held in with thick rust.

Marc groaned, but he was determined and he kept trying. Reaching between the slats for the screw head was an awkward job and after five minutes his shoulder ached and his only achievement was a bloody thumb.

As the knife slipped for the umpteenth time, Marc gave one of the glass slats a final, desperate yank. A chunk of mortar dropped from the gap between the brickwork and the rusty frame holding the slats in place.

Marc studied the gap and noticed that the mortar was badly cracked and crumbled away when he dug it with his thumbnail. He lined the point of the knife up with the hole left behind by the mortar and pushed forwards with a stabbing motion. His reward was a shower of dust, but several more stabs enabled him to make a clear hole between the bricks and the metal. Marc smiled as he pushed the knife into the hole and made the plaster crumble using a sawing motion.

Within a minute he'd cleared a twenty-centimetre gap between frame and wall, but he was making noise, so he decided to stop and make sure he hadn't caught anyone's attention. After jumping down and sweeping the loose dust from what was now a filthy set of clothes, he walked back towards the street and peered through the hedge.

A couple of men were trudging up the hill and, judging by their rough appearance, they were heading for the Dormitory Raquel. They probably wouldn't have heard, but he gave them time to pass before going back to work.

Before long Marc had chipped out all of the mortar along one side of the window. He gave the metal bar holding the slats an experimental knock. The glass shuddered but the mortar at the opposite end snapped away in chunks.

The whole window was about to crash inside, making a noise that would be heard half a street away. Marc gripped one of the slats, but the combined weight of glass and metal was enough to twist his wrist around painfully, until he dropped the knife and steadied the opposite end with his other hand.

It was awkward, but he pulled the entire window out of the surrounding brickwork and ditched it on top of an overgrown shrub with little more than the sound of rustling branches, followed by a metallic clank. It was quite an achievement, and Marc was pleased.

After grabbing the pigskin bag and hooking it over his

back, he placed his palms against the brick window ledge and pulled his legs up. With the whole window out there was plenty of room to get through, but he didn't fancy dropping head first on to the sink, so he had an awkward time swinging his legs in front of his body so that he could lower himself into the sink boots first.

Following a quick jump out of the bowl, he stumbled one step forwards on the tiled floor and came to a halt in the middle of the bathroom. Elated, but still scared, he turned the tap and, after a few coughs from the plumbing, clean water spluttered out, washing away the remains of the spider's web.

Marc cleaned the grit off his hands and arms, then splashed some water up into his face. He glanced at himself in a circular shaving mirror and was surprised by how filthy he was. It was no wonder that the woman in the café had turned her nose up.

He moved out into the hallway, where he was confronted by a gas boiler and a light switch. The pilot light on the boiler was out, but he'd seen the nuns using a similar system on bath-night at the orphanage and he thought he might be able to figure out how to get it going and get some hot water for a bath. He didn't expect anything when he flicked the light switch, but was startled when three uplighters projected Vs of light along the hallway walls.

The first doorway led into a kitchen. The cupboards were mostly bare, but a few odd tins remained and Marc noted that the writing on some of them was in English. There was also an English packet containing something called Bird's Custard and three tall bottles of HP Sauce.

The living room was large, and sparsely furnished. Marc felt a touch creepy as the dark boards creaked under his boots. He raised some of the dust sheets for a peek and discovered a radio, a collection of ornate vases in a glass cabinet and a bookcase filled with books. Some were French, but the majority were in English and Marc thought this was a good sign because it seemed highly unlikely that an Englishman would be returning to Paris any time soon.

With his skin and clothes filthy from the rain, Marc decided that his first priority was to have a wash. Then he'd put on the spare clothes he'd taken off the line at the orphanage and have a nap, because he was exhausted. When he woke up, he'd go out and buy some food, or perhaps even investigate the cinema he'd seen by the shops.

Everything felt better now that he had somewhere to stay. His problems weren't all over, but the idea that he was free to walk the streets of Paris and see a real movie in a real cinema and come home to sleep in a proper bed seemed impossibly exciting.

The good times would only last until the Germans reached town, but that gave him a few days to make plans and learn some of the life skills he'd need if he was going to survive on his own for any length of time.

Marc unbuttoned his shirt as he walked out into the hallway. Before turning towards the bathroom, he noticed a few letters on the doormat and realised that they would tell him the name of the person whose house he had just broken into.

He picked up the most flamboyant letter – a mint-coloured envelope that contained something stiff, like a greeting card or a party invitation – and read the name out loud.

'Mr Charles Henderson.'

Part Two

14 June 1940 – 15 June 1940

By 11 June the French Government had left Paris and German forces were within ten kilometres of the city. Fearing a bloodbath, citizens continued to pour out and less than half of the population remained.

On the night of the 13th the French Military Command stated that it 'aimed to spare Paris the devastation that defence of the city would involve. We cannot justify the sacrifice of our capital and, as a result, all French forces will withdraw to a new line south of Paris.'

The German Army announced that it would enter Paris from the north-west at noon the following day.

CHAPTER EIGHTEEN

While most of Paris fretted over its destiny, Marc Kilgour had enjoyed the most exciting week of his life. He'd been to the cinema every afternoon, watching *The Wizard of Oz* four times, along with propaganda-packed news bulletins, American westerns and French detective movies. He'd ridden the Metro, visited the Champs Elysées and stood at the base of the Eiffel Tower. He would have gone to the top, but it was closed because of the air raids.

Charles Henderson's home provided him with electric light, cooking gas and hot water. There was even a telephone and he'd briefly considered ringing the orphanage to tease Director Tomas about how he was spending his savings. But Marc didn't know the orphanage number and wasn't sure if the call might somehow give his location away.

He slept on a comfortable bed with Egyptian cotton sheets and after a dodgy start he'd even prepared a couple of reasonable meals. But with the north cut off by Germans and the roads south clogged with refugees and French troops, you had to queue for even the simplest items and armed police stood outside bakeries to stop bread queues from turning violent.

Marc had gradually gained a sense of how much things cost and had worked out that Director Tomas' savings would last him for two to three months; as long as he didn't have to worry about paying rent. Unlike the elderly and impoverished citizens who remained in Paris – the young and wealthy having mostly got out – Marc could afford to eat in cafés, which seemed to be suffering from a lack of customers rather than food.

Waiters also provided rare opportunities for conversation, because the biggest problem with Marc's new lifestyle was loneliness. He never imagined that he'd miss the constant buzz of the orphanage, but he often found himself craving a friend and when he was alone in the house he voiced his most poignant thoughts to an imaginary Jae Morel.

The air raids were worst at night, but mostly concentrated on the city centre. Cafés and cinemas were forced to shut at six o'clock, so he spent most evenings reading in Henderson's living room, with the bay window open and occasional interruptions from insects flying inside from the overgrown garden.

Marc had always enjoyed books, but there were none at the orphanage and even when he had a reading book from school he could only find peace to read in the fields out back. So far he'd got through two of Henderson's French novels and struggled with an antique book of folk tales written in German.

Marc knew a fair amount of the language thanks to a half-German schoolmaster who'd given his brightest pupils after-school tuition. The passages Marc couldn't understand were easily filled in by studying the beautiful illustrations, which came in full colour and were embossed with gold and silver leaf. Unfortunately, most of Henderson's books were in English and Marc didn't understand a word of it.

*

Henderson's bedroom contained a double bed that seemed impossibly luxurious compared to the dusty, pee-stained excuses for beds at the orphanage. But best of all was the fact that he didn't have Director Tomas whacking him on the arse if he didn't jump out of bed the instant he was told to.

Freedom was good, Paris was pretty special; but

spending half a morning drooling on a pillow and knowing that you didn't have to get up was the best thing of all. What's more, the Germans had stopped bombing when the French announced the city's surrender, so Marc was enjoying his most peaceful lie-in ever when the house shook with such violence that his skull thumped painfully against the headboard.

A great roar erupted over the brow of the hill and when Marc pulled the curtains he saw a vast, mushroom-shaped fireball towering into the sky. But there were no planes and the explosion was twenty times bigger than any bomb he'd seen up to now.

The heat on the glass was intense, and as Marc heard saucepans clattering downstairs in the kitchen and a glass cabinet toppling in the living room, he was astonished to see a dozen people gathered at the bottom of the hill near the church. They held hands over brows to shield the glare, but looked oddly calm – as if they were watching a firework display, rather than facing the random threat of an air raid.

Alarmed and mystified, Marc pulled on his trousers and boots before buttoning his shirt and bounding downstairs. More blasts erupted as he glanced into the living room and confirmed his worst fears about the cabinets.

Although the spare house-key Marc found in

Henderson's study meant he could now use the front door, he still had no right to be in the house and he steered clear of the neighbours.

After ducking under the hedges enveloping the front gate, he looked to the top of the hill and saw that many of the men from the Dormitory Raquel also stood in the street, watching the receding flames. Smaller explosions continued to rumble, and it was fortunate that the wind was carrying the plumes of smoke away from them.

Running might attract undue attention, so Marc walked briskly downhill, patting his pockets for change to make sure that he had enough for an early lunch or late breakfast. Even though, on his daily trips to the cinema, he passed the café whose owner had directed him towards the Dormitory Raquel, he'd never eaten there again because he'd discovered a little place run by an Italian family not far from the church. The food was much better and Livia – the owner's teenaged daughter – had huge breasts.

Livia, her father, her grandmother and several customers lined up in front of the café, admiring the flames.

'Marc,' the elderly grandmother said, smiling brightly. 'How's your uncle today?'

Café Roma was frequented by locals, and the first time Marc went inside he'd mentioned that he was staying with a sick uncle, deliberately remaining vague about exactly where he lived. Marc wasn't proud of the lie, but the old woman called him a *little trooper* and never missed an opportunity to overfill his plate or give him a free glass of her chocolate mousse.

Marc would happily have exchanged all of the mousse in Paris for a single smile from her well-endowed granddaughter, but all Livia ever did was slam down plates and scowl at Marc like he was something stuck on her shoe.

'My uncle isn't too bad today,' Marc said, as he tried desperately to remember yesterday's lie so that he didn't repeat it. 'I gave him a shave and helped him in the bath.'

'Oh, aren't you a darling?' the old lady said, with her ripe Italian accent. 'I've made a fresh batch of meatballs and spaghetti. Would you like to try?'

'It's not even eleven,' the owner noted, but Marc didn't mind at all. At first he'd been wary of anything beyond the basic soups and stews he'd lived on all his life at the orphanage, but all the food he'd been served in the Café Roma was good, and longstanding connections with local markets and wholesalers meant that the café remained well stocked despite the food shortages.

'So what's going on over the hill?' Marc asked, pointing at the flames.

'The surrender,' the café owner explained. 'Didn't you know? The Germans will enter the city at noon.'

Marc nodded. 'I heard that on on the radio last night. So why are the Germans still bombing?'

'That's you French, not the Germans,' the old lady explained. 'They're letting the Boche have Paris, complete with all the bridges across the Seine, but even the French Command isn't dopy enough to hand the Germans their ammunition factories.'

'Ahhh,' Marc said, as realisation dawned. 'I was sleep— erm . . . I had my uncle in the bath, so I've not heard any news this morning. What else are they saying?'

'Not much,' the owner said. The sky was still darkened with smoke but the fireball from the massive explosion was burning itself out. The old lady took up the answer to Marc's question as Livia's dad followed the first of his customers back inside the cramped café.

'The army has closed all roads out of Paris to civilians so they can get their equipment out, and the Germans have promised to enter the city in a dignified manner and harm nobody,' the old lady said. Then her lips thinned and she tossed curls of grey hair off her face. 'I guess we'll know in an hour.'

CHAPTER NINETEEN

Tours was on the main route between Paris and the south. A few well-placed bombs here could disrupt road and rail traffic through central France and force military supplies and troops to divert hundreds of kilometres through the countryside, causing delay and wasting increasingly scarce fuel supplies.

Ten days of intense bombing had turned the heart of the town into hell, destroying more than a third of the buildings, taking out all of the major bridges and cutting off supplies of gas, water and electricity. There wasn't an unbroken window within two kilometres of the town centre.

But you didn't have to venture far into the surrounding countryside for all signs of war to vanish. Rosie and Paul had found refuge in a small farmhouse belonging to a retired priest and his spinster sister. At this moment, Rosie was running at full pelt across a meadow, gaining ground on Hugo, who wore a headdress made from a piece of knotted rag and chicken feathers.

'Can't get me!' Hugo shouted. But he shrieked as he looked behind and saw that Rosie was almost within touching distance.

'Gotcha, monster,' Rosie growled, as she grabbed the small boy around the waist and hoisted him high into the air with his legs kicking frantically.

Hugo was grinning and breathless as she put him down. 'Again?' he asked.

Rosie liked playing with Hugo because it gave her a chance to act stupid and forget about all the bad stuff. The trouble was, he never wanted to stop.

'OK,' Rosie said, putting her hands over her eyes. 'One last time.'

'*Three* more times,' Hugo demanded.

'Once more, or not at all. I've played with you for nearly an hour.'

'OK . . .' the boy huffed, before spinning around and darting off into the long grass.

'One, two, three . . .' Rosie counted, but gave up the pretence once Hugo was out of earshot. It was too hot for all this running around and she was getting a stitch down her side.

She looked across the meadow and immediately noticed Hugo's head peeking over the top of the ditch. But she knew if she found Hugo too quickly he'd insist on playing again, so she looked mystified for a few moments before starting to stroll towards the ditch.

Hugo sprang up and protested when Rosie got close. 'You peeked!'

'So what?' Rosie teased. 'What are you gonna do about it, titch?'

'You're ugly!' Hugo shouted, before scrambling up the side of the ditch. 'And you smell like horse bum.'

Rosie growled dramatically. 'Oh, you're gonna get it now.'

Hugo shrieked with delight as he pushed through a hedge and began running up a dirt track. When Rosie got through the hedge – a task far more difficult for a burly thirteen year old than for a boy of six – she was alarmed to see Hugo's little legs running at full pelt up a steep path covered with rocks.

'You be careful,' Rosie said. 'Come back and play on the grass.'

'Can't get me,' was Hugo's response.

Rosie didn't fancy bashing her knee on a rock, so she kept her pace down to a brisk walk. Hugo stopped running and looked back with his hands on his hips.

'Come *on*, Rosie, you're not playing properly.'

Hugo cut off the path and dived behind a clump of bushes. A second later he screamed out, 'OWWWWW!'

Rosie envisaged grazed skin and streaks of blood and ran desperately towards Hugo. But by the time she'd made ten metres she heard Hugo say, 'What are you hiding up here for?' in a voice that showed no sign of distress.

Rosie rounded the bushes and saw that Hugo had turned the corner and tripped over her brother's outstretched legs. Paul was sitting against the trunk of a small tree, with his sketchbook and the wooden case containing his drawing pens and inks on the grass at his side.

'Are you OK?' Rosie asked brightly, when she saw her brother. 'What are you doing?'

Paul wiggled his sketchpad. 'Flower arranging,' he tutted.

Rosie wouldn't usually have stood any lip from her brother, but he'd taken their father's death hard and had been even quieter than usual in the week since.

'What are you drawing?' Hugo asked.

'Nothing,' Paul said.

Hugo stepped closer to Paul. 'Please show me,' he begged.

Paul clutched the pad close to his chest, but Hugo

made a grab and Paul shoved him away angrily. 'It's private.'

Hugo tumbled back three steps before falling hard on his bum.

'Careful, moron,' Rosie yelled. 'He's only six.'

Hugo stood up with his bottom lip rolled out like he was going to cry.

'I didn't ask you to come barging over here,' Paul said indignantly. 'I just want to be on my own.'

'I just asked to see your picture,' Hugo said.

Paul grabbed a corner of his pad with his inky fingers and flung it into the dirt. Hugo stared at it, unable to grasp what it was, but Rosie instantly recognised her father's face. One side was an almost perfect drawing, but the other appeared twisted, with the eyeball sunk into the skull and a gaping wound filled with maggots in his cheek.

'You little sicko,' Rosie shouted. 'Why have you got to draw him like that? Why can't you do a nice picture?'

Paul scowled at his sister. 'Because I don't feel like making a *nice* picture, fatso.'

Rosie wasn't fat, but she was sensitive about her stocky build and calling her fat was the easiest way to make her mad.

'I can't look at that,' Rosie shouted, picking the pad off the floor, tearing off the page and ripping the drawing to shreds. She'd expected Paul to fight her, but he didn't move.

'Can you go now you're done interfering?' Paul said calmly.

If Paul had put up a fight Rosie would have felt OK about ripping up the drawing, but the way he sat there, staring pathetically, made her feel terrible. The drawing must have taken hours.

'I'm sorry,' Rosie said sheepishly, as the wind picked up squares of torn paper.

'If you say so,' Paul said.

Rosie felt like her brother was dead inside. She wanted to grab him and thump him until he came back to life.

'Can't you at least talk to me?' Rosie begged. 'I'm hurting too, you know. What is it you want?'

'We should have gone south, like we agreed in the first place,' Paul said. 'Not stayed here with Father Doran and his sister.'

'It's safe here,' Rosie groaned. 'People were dying on the roads, Paul. Probably still are. Here we've got good food, clean water, somewhere decent to sleep . . .'

Paul shook his head. 'Dad's last words were *Find Henderson, give him the papers*. And what are we doing? Sitting on our arses, drawing pictures and playing with six year olds.'

'Dad would have wanted us to be safe more than

anything else,' Rosie said. 'We've been through his pocket book. We've been through every one of the documents in the briefcase, looking for a reference to Henderson, and there's nothing. No phone number, no address, no details of who he works for.'

'But people in England would know, Rosie. If we went south and got a boat to England we could contact someone and find Henderson's assistant: Miss McAfferty.'

'Probably,' Rosie said. 'But even if we make it to Bordeaux – two hundred kilometres on foot, and in this heat – how can we be sure that there's a boat leaving for England? If there *is* a boat, you can bet your life that there are going to be thousands of refugees trying to get on board.'

Paul shrugged. 'I didn't say it would be easy, but I know Dad would have wanted us to try.'

'No,' Rosie said, shaking her head. 'Dad was off his head when he said that. He was bleeding to death. And besides, what about Mum? I know for a fact that she would have wanted us to stay here, where it's safe.'

Paul's silence was as close as he'd get to admitting that Rosie was probably right.

'I'm hungry,' Hugo said, grabbing Rosie's wrist and giving it a tug.

'I'm going back to the cottage,' Rosie said, as she

looked down at Hugo. 'Yvette should have lunch ready soon. Are you coming with us?'

'I suppose,' Paul said reluctantly, snapping the wooden box of ink and drawing pens shut and clambering out of the grass.

CHAPTER TWENTY

Marc had got used to the sight of French troops. Unshaven, underfed and frequently drunk; their uniforms didn't fit and their horse-drawn artillery seemed like a relic from a different age. Germany was only a few hundred kilometres away, but their army seemed to come from another world.

The first columns entering Paris were led by motorcycles and sidecars, followed by senior staff sitting in open-topped Kübelwagens[4] with swastika flags draped across the bonnet. A soothing French voice came out of a megaphone, urging citizens of Paris to stay calm and stand clear of the troops.

---

[4]Kübelwagen – an open-topped German car, similar to a British Land Rover or American Jeep.

Then came infantry. Marching in step, immaculately dressed – from green helmets down to polished boots. Marc stood close enough to the kerb to get a whiff of the superbly groomed horses. Tank tracks left their mark in sunbaked tarmac and polluted the air with a haze of diesel fumes.

The German forces seemed to sweat raw power. It was the most impressive thing Marc had ever seen and he was completely awed. He'd often dreamed of running away to fight for France, but now France was on its knees, and he wanted to swap sides.

Marc could imagine himself in the smart Nazi uniform, commanding his own tank as it smashed buildings and slaughtered anyone stupid enough to defy him. He'd been on the losing end his whole life and this brazen display of strength intoxicated him.

He turned to face the café owner, but instead found himself staring at his daughter Livia.

'Some of them are *so* good looking,' Livia said enthusiastically. 'That uniform . . . *oooh là-là!*'

It was the first time Livia had ever shown Marc anything other than a sneer, and her attraction to German soldiers made him even keener to join up.

'Do you think they'll let French boys join?' he asked. 'When I'm older, obviously.'

A wiry man who often sat in the Café Roma smoking

a cigar and drinking Espresso shocked Marc by cracking him around the back of the head.

'Think of France,' he said bitterly. 'These are your enemies. These are the ones who drop bombs on us. In Poland they rape the women and treat the people like cattle. Our time will come.'

Marc was affronted at being hit by a man who'd never even spoken to him, but he remembered the sad look that crossed Jae Morel's face whenever her two missing brothers were mentioned. On the other hand, Marc didn't feel very patriotic. What had France ever done for him?

'Blond hair and blue eyes,' Livia said, as she looked at Marc. 'You'd make a good little Aryan soldier.'

Marc wasn't sure what Aryan meant, but he was excited by the sudden communication with Livia.

'I expect they'll take all the French boys they can get when they want to fight the British Empire,' the wiry man said. 'The Führer's not fussy about whose blood he spills.'

Another huge column of troops had rounded the corner and Marc was annoyed that the wiry man was killing the mood. Livia seemed almost to read Marc's mind.

'Buzz off, you old misery,' she said. 'Nobody's interested in what you've got to say. Would you rather they came through like this – or blowing up

Paris, one street at a time?'

Affronted, the man turned to walk away, but before he did he scowled at Livia. 'I fought in the last war,' he spat. 'Italian fascists! I suppose you've been on their side all along.'

Marc and Livia exchanged a look, as if to say *What's his problem?*

*

An hour later, Marc was back in the house. He'd stood Henderson's glass-fronted cabinet back up, but the collection of vases was smashed to pieces. He switched the radio on and listened to the BBC French service reporting on the orderly occupation of Paris and rumours that the French Government had begun negotiating surrender for the rest of France.

In contrast, Radio France continued to portray the surrender of Paris as a tactical withdrawal and boldly predicted a counterstrike that would sweep the Germans from French soil. Marc was twelve years old and he'd led a sheltered life, but even he could tell it was propaganda of the feeblest sort.

It was a warm day and Marc sat in an armchair with his shirt thrown on the floor beside him. When the news turned to music he closed his eyes and became engrossed in his tank commander fantasy: conquering countries in his smart German uniform by day and conquering pretty girls like Livia by night. Hitler would award him medals for bravery. He'd have a pretty wife in the country and a mistress or two in the city. One day he'd return to Beauvais in his officer's uniform with a massive horse whip. He'd haul Director Tomas into the village centre and thrash him until he passed out. Then he'd run over the old fool's legs in his tank.

The thought of Director Tomas with squashed legs made Marc laugh aloud. But his mirth was curtailed by a thunderous knock on the front door. He dived out of the armchair and crawled up to the bay window, where three men stood on the doorstep. One wore a pale suit, the other two wore the black uniform of the Gestapo – Hitler's feared secret police.

When they didn't get a response, the younger Gestapo officer ripped a pistol out of his holster and shot the lock off the front door. Marc jumped with fright, then switched off the radio and ran into the hallway as one of the Germans barged the front door open with his shoulder. This forced him to double back and squeeze into a gap between the wall and an armchair.

'Henderson has left for the south,' the man in plain clothes said irritably to one Gestapo officer, as another ran to search upstairs. 'He knows we compromised all the leave-behinds in France. He's got no reason to remain in Paris.'

'*No,*' the Gestapo officer said firmly. 'Henderson will remain and try to set up a new spy network. I've questioned the British suspects myself and they all say that he's most determined.'

'Questioned – or *tortured?*' the plain clothes man snorted. 'People just say what you want to hear if you push them like that.'

'I know my job, Herr Potente,' the Gestapo officer snapped. 'This is no longer your command. *I* have orders to run counter-intelligence operations in occupied Paris, and Henderson is our top priority.'

A second crash came at the rear of the house, as a Gestapo officer who'd been sent around the back kicked in a door and entered the kitchen.

'Herr Oberst[5],' the black-uniformed man said, clicking his heels obediently and giving a Nazi salute. 'Nobody tried escaping out the back. The houses on either side appear to be unoccupied.'

'There's nobody upstairs either,' the other officer added, as he ran back down the stairs. 'But the bed is ruffled, as if it was slept in recently, and there are damp clothes hanging over the bath – either a boy or a very small man. I'd say they were washed out late last night or early this morning.'

---

[5]Oberst – a high-ranking German officer.

Marc's heart thumped as the four men stood in the doorway less than five metres away.

'A boy,' the Oberst said, stroking his chin curiously. 'Find the boy, and whatever neighbours you can. Interrogate them. Use force if necessary, but our orders are to behave as gentlemen until the occupation of Paris is complete. So if you have to make a mess, make sure you clean it up.'

'Yes, Herr Oberst,' the officer said, before heading out of the front door and calling to a couple of regular soldiers who now stood by the front gate.

'We must search carefully,' Herr Potente said, warning the two officers. 'When we captured the British spies we found several booby traps. One of my men lost three fingers when a filing cabinet blew up on him.'

The Oberst nodded. 'Then be careful everyone, but don't waste time. Obergruppenführer Heydrich is taking a personal interest in the Mannstein affair. He's extremely unhappy that Digby Clarke made it out of Paris.'

'I spoke with Mannstein at the hotel late last night,' Potente said. 'He's disappointed that his drawings were stolen by Clarke, but he says he'll be able to recreate them within weeks.'

'But we don't want the British getting the plans out of France,' the Oberst shouted. 'And I want Henderson before he can recruit new spies. If we don't capture Henderson, Clarke *and* the plans, I'm going to make sure that your next posting is a very unpleasant one, Herr Potente. Is that understood?'

'Yes, Herr Oberst,' Potente said, giving a Nazi salute as the Gestapo officer backed out of the room.

Marc was terrified. He could only understand about half of the Germans' conversation, but he'd picked up enough to realise that they were prepared to torture him for information.

CHAPTER TWENTY-ONE

Father Doran and his sister Yvette still worked two acres of land around the small farmhouse in which they'd been born more than seventy years earlier. The Father had been parish priest for almost half a century and was one of the most respected men in the area. It had surprised nobody when the elderly siblings took in three orphans and several neighbours had offered help, especially for Hugo, who'd arrived with nothing but the clothes on his back.

The Dorans always stopped for two hours in the middle of the day and ate a large meal made from garden vegetables and meat butchered on a nearby farm. After a soup and a main course of beef cooked in a wine sauce, Paul and Rosie struggled through a fruit tart for dessert.

Hugo barely touched the first two courses, reserving all of his available stomach space for afters.

'I have some friends coming around to play cards this afternoon,' Father Doran said, as he dabbed his shrivelled lips on a napkin. 'So you three keep the noise down if you're staying indoors.'

The three kids nodded as they left the table. Rosie went to the sink to help Yvette wash up, while Hugo followed Paul upstairs to the small bedroom shared by all of them. There was a double bed, in which Paul and Rosie slept, and two sofa cushions pushed together on the bare floor for Hugo, although he usually claimed to be scared of the dark and crawled up under the bedcovers to sleep between Rosie and Paul.

'Do you want to play outside?' Hugo asked, as Paul pulled a brown case out from beneath the bed.

'I want to take another look at these papers,' Paul said. 'Dad was always moaning that he had a terrible memory. He *must* have written down contact details for Henderson somewhere.'

'*Please*,' Hugo whined.

'You've just eaten half a tart,' Paul said, as he flipped the suitcase open. 'You'll throw up if you start chasing around now.'

'So boring,' Hugo complained, as he slumped backwards on to the bed beside the case.

Paul perched on the edge of the bed and grabbed his father's pocket book. He'd been through it a dozen times and could now remember the words and numbers before he came to them. Meanwhile, Hugo rummaged inside the case.

'Don't mess all the papers up,' Paul warned, but he saw that Hugo had grabbed his father's cigar tube. Mr Clarke always kept the fat tube case with compartments for six Cuban cigars in his briefcase so that he could offer them to clients. 'Oh. You can play with that if you want,' he added.

As Paul twisted his brains, trying to find something he'd previously missed in the pocket book, Hugo unscrewed the lid on the metal cigar case. He pulled out the largest of the wrapped cigars and placed it between his lips.

'Look, Paul,' Hugo grinned.

Paul tutted. 'I'm trying to concentrate.'

'Why can't kids smoke?' Hugo asked, as he blew imaginary smoke out of his lungs.

'I don't know.' Paul shrugged. 'It's like, adults try to stop kids having all kinds of fun. Rosie lit up one of my dad's cigars once for a dare. She puked *everywhere* and our mum whacked her on the bum with her hairbrush.'

Hugo laughed as he slid the cigar back into its pouch. 'When I'm older I'm gonna smoke fifty cigars and a hundred cigarettes every day.'

'*I* won't,' Paul said. 'I don't like the smell. My dad never smoked.'

'So why did he have cigars?'

'For his clients. My dad said if you give a client a lit cigar, they have to sit still and listen to your sales pitch until they've finished smoking it.'

'What's a pitch?' Hugo asked, as he threw the cigar tube high into the air.

'Hey,' Paul said. 'That belonged to my dad! Don't wreck it.'

But Hugo had already thrown it up again. This time it hit the ceiling and veered wildly off course, hitting the edge of a dresser with a clang before landing on the floorboards.

'Idiot,' Paul said angrily, as he reached over Hugo and grabbed the cigar tube off the floor. 'That's *it* - you're not touching any of my dad's stuff again.'

Hugo turned towards Paul and showered him with spit as he blew a big raspberry in his face.

'Cut it out, Hugo! Do you want me to punch you?'

'I'm going outside,' Hugo sulked, as he slid off the bed. 'This is so boring.'

Hugo thumped down the stairs and Paul sighed as he noticed that the bottom was hanging off the cigar case. He was about to try pushing it back on when he noticed a loose length of insulated wire behind it. When he levered the cap the rest of the way off he unveiled a small blue bulb and another wire that linked to a slim battery.

It was obviously some kind of torch and the switch was built into the lid. But when he turned it on, Paul was disappointed by the fact that it only produced a small bluish dot. This seemed odd, but he could see no reason for hiding a torch unless it was used for something pretty special.

The only thing you can do with a torch is shine it at stuff and, as Paul was looking for a hidden message, he decided to shine it at the pocket book. The first couple of pages produced nothing, but on the third page, several faint blue lines glowed when he shone the light on the writing.

Part of Paul wanted to race downstairs and tell Rosie that he'd discovered something, but she was such a bossy-boots that he decided it would be best to carry on alone. As the glow of the markings was faint in daylight, Paul hitched the bedclothes over his head and tried again in pitch darkness. Now he could see the markings clearly, but they were just scribble. The kind of random lines that you might make if you were trying out a new pen.

There were no further markings on the next three pages, but Paul's heart leaped when the blue light exposed an entire page aglow with his father's handwriting. Names, phone numbers, dates, times and places of meetings. However, no mention of Henderson.

Over the next few pages Paul discovered more notes glowing under the blue light, but none of them seemed to relate to Henderson and he grew increasingly nervous as he got close to the end of the book.

Finally, just a few pages from the end, he found a quickly scrawled note: *Henderson C. home 34451 Embassy 34200.* Paul felt a rush of excitement as he burst out from under the bedcovers and grabbed something to write down the numbers on before he forgot them.

Once they were safely transcribed, he bolted downstairs and waved the piece of paper under Rosie's nose as she dried a roasting tin with a dish cloth.

'Are you joking?' Rosie grinned as she wrapped her wet hands around her brother's back and gave him a hug. 'How did you find that? I'll ask Father Doran where the nearest phone is. We can call him straight away.'

'Father Doran,' Paul shouted, as he ran out of the kitchen and into the living room. 'We've got a number for Mr Henderson.'

The elderly priest had cleared the dining table and set out playing cards and wine glasses for his friends.

'You have?' he smiled.

'I found a torch,' Paul explained. 'It shows up the

hidden writing in my dad's pocket book.'

'Ahhh,' the priest said, wagging his finger knowingly. 'Ultra-violet light. I believe the Vatican used a similar technique for passing messages during the Great War. Well, that's marvellous – assuming that this Henderson is still in Paris.'

'And that the phone lines are working,' Rosie added. 'Paris is behind German lines now. I've got no idea whether we'll be able to get through. We need a phone, Father. Do you know anyone around here who has one?'

'I've never used one myself,' the priest said. 'But there's a vineyard about three kilometres down towards the village. The owner is a widow I've known for many years. I'm sure she'll let you use her phone, if it's working.'

'Great,' Paul said. 'We'll head up there now.'

CHAPTER TWENTY-TWO

'Got him,' the junior officer announced triumphantly, as he dragged Marc from behind the chair. Before the boy knew it he'd been shoved backwards into the armchair and the Oberst loomed over him.

'What is your name?' the black-uniformed Oberst shouted, switching to French that was about as competent as Marc's German.

'David Henri,' Marc lied.

'Do you speak German?'

Marc nodded. 'A little bit.'

'If you understood our conversation, you'll know what I want to hear.'

Marc shook his head meekly. 'All I know is that Henderson lives here, sir. I don't know him. I've never even seen him.'

'Then why are you here?'

'I came from the north,' Marc explained. 'I came here to shelter.'

'All the doors and windows are intact,' the German said. Then he turned towards one of his junior officers. 'I don't believe him. Fetch my bag from the car.'

'I swear it's true, sir. I pulled out the bathroom window. There's still a hole, and you can go and look if you don't believe me.'

Without warning, the Gestapo officer grabbed Marc out of the chair and smacked him hard across the face. 'I *don't* believe you. And you *will* address me as Herr Oberst, is that clear?'

The blow left Marc in a daze, with blood welling in his nostril. He was slow to respond and the Oberst dragged him across the room and knocked the side of his head against the wall.

'I understand, Herr Oberst,' Marc said, seeing stars and fighting tears as the blood dribbled over his top lip.

'Who is Henderson? Where is Henderson?' the Oberst shouted, as he jabbed two fingers into Marc's stomach.

'I swear I don't know.'

The Oberst looked at one of the junior officers. 'Check the bathroom window, then search the house for his things.'

The officer clicked his heels and headed out as his colleague returned with a leather doctor's bag. The bag jangled as the officer placed it on a tabletop.

'Pliers,' the Oberst ordered. 'Then hold the boy around the neck.'

Marc could hardly stand after the beating and put up no fight as the junior officer stood close behind him and wrapped an arm around his neck.

'This is your last chance to tell me about Henderson,' the Oberst warned, as he rested the cold pliers against the squashy tip of Marc's nose.

Marc considered inventing something to satisfy the Oberst, but he knew a lie would only lead him into deeper trouble and his head was too fuzzy to come up with anything convincing.

'I swear I don't know anything,' he said, crying now as his blood soaked into the junior officer's sleeve.

'We shall see,' the Oberst said, pinching Marc's nostrils shut, forcing him to open his mouth.

'Please,' Marc begged, as the arm tightened at his throat.

The Oberst pushed the open pliers into Marc's mouth and clamped one of his upper front teeth. Blood flowed as the Oberst twisted the pliers, accompanied by a pain beyond any Director Tomas had ever inflicted on him. The tooth made a shocking crunch as the Oberst twisted it out of Marc's jaw, then it hit the floor with a delicate clatter.

'I demand you tell me everything,' the Oberst bellowed, as the junior officer released the grip on Marc's neck a little.

'I swear I don't know Henderson,' Marc screamed. His words slurred because his tongue splashed in the blood filling his mouth. 'I just got here. I've never even seen Henderson.'

'Maybe you'll remember something after I pull some more teeth.'

'Please no,' Marc sobbed. 'I never did anything. I'm nothing to do with Henderson.'

The other junior officer came back into the room, holding Marc's pigskin bag and damp clothes.

'Herr Oberst,' the officer said brusquely, 'the bathroom window *is* missing. There's nothing belonging to a boy in the house, except what fits inside this bag. He also has a large sum of money.'

The Oberst looked at the rolled-up francs, then back at Marc who was turning blue from blocked nostrils and the arm around his neck.

'That's a lot of money,' the Oberst said. 'Did you find it here?'

Marc shook his head. 'It's mine.'

The Oberst cracked a huge smile. 'Not now it isn't,' he

said, as he tucked the money into his tunic. Then he turned towards his three colleagues. 'We'll eat and drink like kings tonight,' he joked. 'I think our young friend is telling the truth. Let him go.'

Marc hit the floor with a thump as the junior officer released the stranglehold. He inhaled blood as he fought for breath, and coughed violently as the Oberst stepped over him.

'If you speak to anyone about Gestapo business I'll find you and I'll kill you *very* slowly,' the Oberst warned.

Marc sobbed with pain as he stared up at the four laughing Nazis. He felt idiotic as he remembered his fantasy of just a few minutes earlier. People like him didn't command German tanks – they got crushed by them.

Unlike the Oberst, Herr Potente didn't enjoy seeing a twelve-year-old boy beaten up, and had stepped outside to smoke.

'Let me guess,' Potente said, wincing as he stepped through the arched doorway and saw Marc's bare torso covered with blood. 'The boy is a refugee. He knows nothing.'

The Oberst rose up on his heels and shouted impatiently, 'Herr Potente, if you are *such* an expert, kindly explain why your men let Henderson and Clarke disappear in the first place?'

The Oberst was a powerful man and Potente didn't

speak as frankly as he would have liked to. 'Your Gestapo will have hundreds of men in Paris, Herr Oberst. I had just six, and I was working behind enemy lines. I regret that we didn't succeed, but our options and resources were extremely limited.'

The Oberst dismissed the argument with a flick of his hand. 'I must leave now. I have to find a suitable building and establish a Gestapo headquarters. You mentioned an excellent hotel, didn't you, Potente?'

'Yes, Herr Oberst,' Potente said. 'The Hotel Etalon in the eighth arrondissement. I've been staying there with Mannstein and the facilities are excellent.'

'I see,' the Oberst said. 'Perhaps I shall commandeer Hotel Etalon for the Gestapo. When I was in Austria I found that hotel rooms became cells and interrogation suites with minimal conversion.'

'What about this house?' the officer who'd been holding Marc asked. 'Shall we keep watch in case Henderson returns?'

The Oberst thought for a second. 'I agree with Potente. There's no reason for Henderson to come back. But station a lookout in the next house for a few days, just in case.'

'And the boy?'

The Oberst looked down at Marc and shrugged. 'There's no need to kill him. Let him stay here a while to find his feet, then turf him out.'

'Very good, Herr Oberst,' the officer said, saluting.

As the Oberst turned to leave, the telephone standing on the bureau rang out. Potente rushed across and crouched in front of the microphone, before grabbing the earpiece from its hook.

'*Hello*,' Potente said, speaking in French, whilst making a fair stab at an English accent. '*Charles Henderson speaking.*'

*

Rosie stood in the hallway of a large house, with a curved staircase behind and a stag's head mounted on the wall above her head.

'Is it Henderson?' Paul whispered impatiently.

Rosie smiled and nodded before shushing her brother. 'Mr Henderson! Thank god it's you,' she said. 'You don't know me, but I believe you knew my father, Digby Clarke?'

'Very well indeed,' Herr Potente said warmly.

'My father was killed in an air raid last week. The last thing he did was ask us to try and find you.'

'I see,' Potente said, struggling not to sound too excited. 'I'm sorry for your loss; your father was a good man and a great servant of his country.'

'Thank you,' Rosie said politely.

'Now. I believe your father had some important

documents. Do you know of their whereabouts?'

'Yes,' Rosie said happily. 'That's exactly why we're contacting you. We've kept all of the blueprints and documents relating to Mannstein's radio. We were trying to get south to put them on a boat at Bordeaux, but all our petrol got stolen and—'

'Where are you now . . .?' Suddenly Potente realised he ought to sound sympathetic. 'I'm sorry; you have had a terrible time this past week. You must be Digby's daughter. It's Rosie, isn't it?'

'That's right, Mr Henderson,' Rosie said, nodding. 'We're just outside Tours, staying with a retired priest. It's comfortable, but we'll try heading south again with the documents if that's what you want.'

'No,' Potente said sharply. 'The roads are still dangerous. And I take it you have no transport?'

'None,' Rosie confirmed. 'Although the priest looking after us seems well connected. He might be able to sort something out . . .'

'There's no need to trouble him,' Potente said. 'I'm in Paris, and so the front line now lies between us. I'm sure I can find a way through, but it may be a day or two before I can reach you.'

'And what then?' Rosie asked. 'Will you be able to get us on a boat to England?'

'Absolutely,' Potente said, smoothly. 'Now, the phone

lines could go down at any time, so I must have the address of the farm where you're staying. Just sit tight and don't worry about a thing. You're *completely* safe.'

*

Marc lay on the floor with a mouthful of blood as Herr Potente put the telephone receiver down and grinned at the Oberst.

'Fate has turned in our favour,' he smiled, as he waved the notebook on which he'd written the address of the farm.

'Luck,' the Oberst spat fiercely. 'I don't like to rely on luck. You should have been monitoring calls to this house all along.'

Potente shook his head with frustration. 'It wasn't possible while the city was under French control. I only had six men under my command—'

'Yes, yes,' the Oberst interupted impatiently. 'I've heard your excuses already. What are you planning to do now?'

Potente thought for a second. 'The problem is, the documents are behind French lines. If their army regroups outside Paris . . .'

'Regroups!' The Oberst laughed. 'The French Army has nothing left to regroup. The only thing holding up our advance are retreating French troops clogging the roads.'

'I'll need a car and some fuel to go up to the front line,' Potente said.

'Very well,' the Oberst said, nodding. 'Herr Schmidt will organise it. Now I must head for this Hotel Etalon. I'll arrange for Mannstein to be transported to Poland and inform him that he'll be reunited with his blueprints within a few days.'

Potente looked confused. 'I thought a production facility was being constructed for Mannstein in Germany?'

The Oberst shook his head with utter contempt. 'Don't be an idiot! Mannstein is a Jew. The SS has special facilities for Jewish scientists and researchers in Poland.'

'I don't think he'll like that,' Potente said. 'We've negotiated an agreement for facilities in Hamburg. Mannstein's name may sound Jewish but he's married to a Catholic, so he's a lapsed Jew at worst . . .'

'I'm sure that the SS guards will ensure Mannstein adapts to his new home.' The Oberst smiled. 'And I don't intend to debate Gestapo policy with a junior Abwehr officer. Is that clear, Herr Potente?'

'Of course, Herr Oberst,' Potente said, resignedly. 'One final question. What would you like me to do with Clarke's children once I've recaptured the documents?'

The Oberst shrugged. 'They might know something

about Henderson, so make sure they're properly interrogated. Then kill them.'

CHAPTER TWENTY-THREE

Marc woke up to find the room dark and a man gently slapping his cheek to bring him around. The roof of his mouth was lined with clotted blood.

'Keep calm,' the man looming above him said soothingly. 'Drink some of this.'

Marc propped himself on his elbow and spotted his bloody tooth on the boards in front of him. He grabbed an enamel cup from the man and quickly downed several mouthfuls of water. He felt groggy and the hole in his gum throbbed with pain.

'Who are you?' Marc asked, eyeing the stocky man with a scruffy beard.

'The name's Henderson,' he said. 'Charles Henderson.'

Marc felt a touch worried at this. He'd broken into

the man's house and pretty much helped himself to everything.

'The Germans are looking for you,' Marc croaked, as Henderson helped him to sit up. 'There's someone next door . . .'

Henderson drew a line across his throat and made a choking noise. 'Not now there isn't,' he said, smiling. 'So has my house been to your liking? You must have been here for a week now.'

Marc was surprised. 'If you knew, why didn't you turf me out?'

'I've been busy,' Henderson said, showing off a nice row of teeth when he smiled. He was a good-looking man, but he badly needed a shave and shampoo. 'And your being here made it look like I'd skipped town.'

As Henderson said this, he pulled a hip flask out of his jacket and unscrewed the cap. 'Whisky,' he explained, as he handed it to Marc. 'Rinse your mouth with it. You probably won't like the taste, but it's a natural disinfectant and the alcohol might help numb the pain.'

Marc's eyes were blurred with tears and his hands were shaking. Henderson gave him a damp cloth to wipe his face.

'The Germans who did this – did you overhear anything?'

'All sorts.' Marc nodded. 'I'm not sure I remember all of it.'

'Try your best. Start from the beginning.'

'There was something about leave-behinds and Mannstein,' Marc said. 'My German isn't exactly perfect. It seems so fast when *they* speak it.'

'That's OK,' Henderson said softly. 'I know you're hurting, but please try and tell me as much as you can.'

Marc accidentally swallowed a sip of whisky and broke out in a coughing fit.

'Don't worry,' Henderson said. 'It doesn't matter if you swallow a few drops. You're in shock; it might even help calm you down.'

'I don't know what a *leave-behind* is, but they're all compromised – or something,' Marc said.

Henderson nodded. 'Bad business.'

'What are they?' Marc asked.

'Once British intelligence knew the Germans were going to take control of France, we started recruiting agents who'd stay and work behind enemy lines. We don't know how – a double agent, torture or whatever – but the Germans got hold of the names and addresses of every British agent working in Europe, including mine.

'The Nazis captured and killed more than two dozen agents when they invaded Belgium and Holland. Our people in France had time to escape, but our cupboard is now bare. As far as I'm aware, I'm the only operational agent left in France.'

'Sounds bad,' Marc said, nodding.

'What about Mannstein?' Henderson asked. 'You said his name cropped up.'

'They mentioned a hotel where he was staying. The Etalon, I think. And the Oberst – the head Gestapo guy – he said he was going there to commandeer the hotel.'

Henderson sounded excited. 'The Oberst! Oberst Hinze was here?'

Marc shrugged. 'They just called him Oberst.'

'Tall guy,' Henderson said. 'Slicked back hair and a funny kind of lump on the side of his neck?'

'That's him exactly,' Marc said. 'He's the bastard who ripped my tooth out.'

'You're lucky that's all he did,' Henderson said. 'He's a nasty piece of work. Mind you, you can say that about most of the men you see in a black uniform.'

'Why black?' Marc asked.

'Green uniforms are worn by ordinary German soldiers. Most of them were called up to fight for Germany just like French and British boys were called up to fight for the allies. Black uniform is the SS. That's the elite Nazi regiments, which includes the Gestapo. They're fanatics. Hardcore Nazis who answer only to Hitler.'

'He certainly strutted round here like he owned the place,' Marc said.

'And Mannstein is at the Hotel Etalon?'

'That's what they said.'

Henderson smiled. 'That's one of the most useful pieces of information I've heard all week. What else?'

'There was a phone call as they were leaving. Some kids in Tours, trying to contact you.'

Henderson looked mystified. 'I don't know any kids.'

'Potente pretended that he was you. They were talking about plans and he was going down south to meet them or something.'

'Digby Clarke?' Henderson asked.

Marc nodded. 'Yeah, they mentioned that name. He's dead apparently. It was his daughter that telephoned and Potente is going down to this place in Tours to collect the plans and interrogate his kids about you.'

Henderson slapped his hands against his cheeks. 'Shit,' he shouted, standing up and lashing out at a waste-paper basket. 'I can't believe Clarke's dead. Shit, shit, shit, *shit*.

'We can't stay here,' he continued – calmer, but only slightly. 'If the Gestapo find the guard I killed they'll kill you out of spite, along with anyone else who happens to be in the neighbourhood. How are your legs? Are you up for a walk?'

'My mouth's throbbing, but there's nothing wrong with my legs,' Marc said, as he leaned on the side of an armchair and pulled himself off the floor. He felt light-headed, but he was starting to get control over his shaking hands.

'I have to go to the Hotel Etalon and get to Mannstein,' Henderson said, thinking aloud. 'Then get down to Tours and find those kids before Potente gets hold of them.'

'Maybe I can help,' Marc said determinedly. 'I can't stay here and they've stolen all my money.'

'You look pretty tough,' Henderson said uncertainly. 'And I could do with a hand, but . . .'

'They ripped out my tooth,' Marc spat. 'Give me a gun and I'll blow their bastard heads off.'

'It's not a game, kid. The Gestapo kill people like *that*,' Henderson said, clicking his fingers for effect. 'I can give you a couple of thousand francs and drop you off somewhere across town. The way things are you should find another empty house easily enough.'

'I never did anything to them,' Marc continued. 'I want to get them back. I know I'm just a kid, but I'm clever. I won't mess up, I swear.'

Henderson sucked air between his teeth as he weighed up Marc's offer. He didn't like the idea of putting a boy in danger, but he was exhausted and didn't fancy entering Gestapo headquarters alone.

'If the Gestapo catch you they'll torture you, then stick

you up against a post and shoot you through the head,' Henderson warned.

Marc smiled awkwardly. 'We'd better not get caught then.'

'OK . . .' Henderson said, half smiling. 'Let me think for a few seconds. The Gestapo have only just arrived in town, and that's our main advantage. Potente is the only one who knows what I look like and he's gone south to Tours. With luck we can sneak into the hotel, find Mannstein's room and kill him.'

'I thought we'd be helping him to escape,' Marc gasped.

Henderson shook his head. 'We've already negotiated with Mannstein and invited him back to Britain. He chose to work with the Nazis and he won't change his mind now.'

'That was another thing that got mentioned,' Marc said. 'They've told Mannstein that he's going to Hamburg, but Oberst Hinze is actually sending him to some place in Poland.'

'A special labour camp, most likely.' Henderson nodded. 'Clarke and I told Mannstein that the Nazis would never treat a French Jew with any kind of respect, but he didn't believe us. He's like an awful lot of people who get taken in by Nazi promises, whilst turning a blind eye to the fact that they're a bunch of racist thugs.'

Henderson reached above his bookcase and opened a hidden flap. Beneath it were two bolts, which enabled the entire bookcase to roll forwards on castors when they were released.

'Blimey.' Marc smiled as he took another sip of whisky. 'I never knew it did that.'

'I came back because of this lot, not out of concern for you,' Henderson admitted, as he grabbed the wooden dado rail halfway up the wall and lifted out a perfectly disguised panel, behind which a three-shelved compartment was built into the wall.

'Is that gold?' Marc asked, as he eyed a stack of shining ingots. But before he got an answer his gaze was drawn towards cardboard boxes filled with ammunition and three guns hanging from hooks.

'Sten gun,' Henderson said, as he pulled one out and showed it to Marc. 'Not the most accurate weapon, but if you've got five seconds and you need to kill everyone in a room it's bloody handy. Mind you, this is more useful for what we're doing.'

Henderson pulled out an automatic pistol with a silencer screwed on the front. 'I'm going to be using this,' Henderson said. 'I'll give you the Sten, but it's a weapon of last resort because half of Paris will hear all about it when you pull the trigger on that thing.'

'What about the gold?' Marc asked.

'I can't come back here,' Henderson said, 'so I'm taking everything. There's about a hundred thousand francs in French currency, but the Boche might bring in their own and make it worthless. On the other hand, gold never goes out of fashion.'

'It's lucky the Germans didn't find this lot,' Marc said. 'I thought they did a pretty thorough search.'

Henderson smiled and pointed up at the ceiling. 'I expect they found the handgun, false passports and ten thousand francs under the skirting upstairs and thought they'd got everything.'

'Dummy stash,' Marc said, nodding as his tongue explored the mound of dry blood that had built up around his missing tooth. 'That's pretty smart.'

'I never should have had to come back here,' Henderson said firmly. '*Smart* would have been moving all this stuff out before the Germans reached Paris. But with everything that's been going on, with thousands of documents at the Embassy to destroy, plus a hundred Embassy staff to evacuate and two dozen agents and their families . . . I don't think I've slept more than three hours at a stretch in the last fortnight.'

'So what now?' Marc asked.

'We're certainly not doing ourselves any favours by standing around here,' Henderson said. 'I'll pack up everything we need. You go to the bathroom, wipe yourself down and put your shirt back on. There should be some pain killers in the bathroom cabinet if you want them. The Germans have announced an eight o'clock curfew, so we'd better get a move on if we want to make it to the Hotel Etalon without getting pulled up at a road block.'

Henderson reached into the wall cavity and pulled out a small tin. He unscrewed the lid and took out a metal phial barely bigger than his thumbnail.

'What's that?' Marc asked, as Henderson dropped it into his bloody palm.

'No spy leaves home without one,' he explained. 'Cyanide capsule. Put the pill in your mouth and crunch it. You'll be dead within twenty seconds.'

'Is it painful?' Marc asked, as he stared dumbly at the metal pill case.

'Less painful than being tortured by Oberst Hinze until your heart gives out.' Henderson shrugged. 'Look, you don't have to come with me. I'll hold nothing against you if you want me to drop you off somewhere instead.'

Marc shook his head determinedly. Henderson struck him as a decent man and for some reason the prospect of the Hotel Etalon and facing the Gestapo scared him far less than the prospect of being dropped on a street corner and left to wander Paris alone.

CHAPTER TWENTY-FOUR

Charles Henderson didn't feel great about having Marc alongside him. Before joining the Espionage Research Unit he'd been a naval intelligence officer and their training course gave strict instructions never to use kids. The intelligence manual said that children were physically weak, untrustworthy, unable to handle stress and liable to panic or scream.

But Marc was the only help on offer and Henderson wasn't ungrateful for it. He'd slept less than ten hours in the past four days. He hadn't washed or eaten a proper meal and was only keeping himself going with strong black coffee and Benzedrine pills. The worst part was knowing that it wasn't over. If Henderson made it out of Hotel Etalon alive, he'd still have to break through the German and French lines and somehow get to Tours ahead of Potente, who was already on the road.

Henderson drove a small Fiat and the clock on the dashboard told him it was just a few minutes until the eight o'clock curfew, though at this time in June there was still plenty of daylight. The roads were dead, except for the odd truck packed with German troops. Most cars had left the city crammed with refugees, and the few remaining drivers didn't want to risk being made into an example by the newly arrived Germans. Everyone had seen newspaper pictures of the corpses hanging from lampposts in Warsaw.

Marc sat in the passenger seat. The mix of adrenaline and whisky made him feel better, and regular beatings at the orphanage had left him with an unusually high pain threshold. He was worried about Henderson though. Sweat poured down the man's face, his driving was crazy and a couple of times his expression glazed over so badly that Marc thought the car was going to end up ploughing into a wall.

They cruised past Hotel Etalon at just six minutes to eight. The private road leading up to its grand lobby was lined with open-topped Kübelwagens and three of the grand Mercedes saloons used by senior German officers.

'There's four regular soldiers guarding the entrance,'

Marc noted, as Henderson turned into a narrow side street and pulled up.

'I saw them,' Henderson said warily.

He stepped out of the tiny car and looked up and down the street. 'We've got to get in there before curfew or we're buggered.'

Henderson took out a duffel bag containing the partially-assembled Sten gun and handed it to Marc.

'How do we get inside?' the boy asked, as the weight of the bag practically wrenched his arm from its socket.

'Every posh hotel has a staff entrance. It'll be around the back.'

'But they might be guarding that too,' Marc said. 'And if we get in, how the hell are we going to get away again when the whole city is under a curfew?'

'Good questions,' Henderson said, as they walked briskly towards the back of the hotel. 'I'll let you know the answers just as soon as I think of them.'

A left turn took them on to a concrete ramp, misted with steam curling out of the hotel kitchen and stinking of the rubbish overflowing from giant metal bins. Three kitchen staff stood in an open doorway smoking cigarettes and a bored-looking German guard sat on a step behind them.

'Act as if we do this every night of our lives,' Henderson said to Marc, as they approached the door.

'Evening, gents,' Henderson said brightly, nodding to the smokers.

They looked a touch mystified, but it was a big hotel and they didn't know everyone who worked there. The German stretched out his leg to stop them and spoke in bad French.

'My French not too good,' Henderson said, pointing jovially towards himself. 'I night porter. My son is shoe-shine.'

The German didn't seem happy to have drawn guard duty on his first night in Paris and he looked up miserably and pointed into the kitchen with his thumb. 'Go ahead.'

Savage heat blasted Marc as he stepped inside. A filthy corridor took them into the hotel kitchen proper, where three men as rough as any Marc had seen leaving the Dormitory Raquel stood in front of a trough, scrubbing massive pots. Another man barged past, carrying a crate filled with empty champagne bottles.

It seemed impossible that anything could be hotter, but as they reached the centre of the kitchen Marc felt as if the sun had crash-landed on his head. It seemed impossible to breathe, let alone work in such heat, but dozens of kitchen staff carted ingredients, chopped, boiled, seared and dragged heavy trays out of ovens.

Marc and Henderson caught a few odd glances, but

nobody had time to stop and ask questions. When the waiters passed through the swinging doors leading into the restaurant they were able to glimpse a room filled with black uniforms. At the far end, someone was making a speech to a chorus of drunken laughter.

'It's good if they're pissed,' Henderson said, smiling as he stepped out of the kitchen into a narrow corridor with great clumps of mildew growing on the walls. 'Remember, Marc: confidence is key. Always look like you know where you're going, even if you haven't got a clue.'

Marc was scared and felt slightly woozy, but at least the corridor was merely stifling, rather than unbearable. They walked twenty metres until they came to a wooden staircase that went down to the hotel basement. A door at the bottom led them into a room containing two giant washing machines. Beyond the machines a woman worked flat out, stretching white hotel sheets over a steam-press, then taking off the flattened sheets and folding them into neat squares.

She stared oddly at Marc and Henderson. Clearly she didn't get many visitors.

'Hello,' Henderson said. 'We just started work here. I'm supposed to unblock a toilet for someone called Mannstein.'

The woman raised a single eyebrow. 'How the hell

does that bring you down here?'

'I just came along the corridor.'

She looked at Marc. 'And you've brought your son to work?'

'Shoe-shine,' Marc said.

'We've never had that before,' the woman said. 'Night porter does the shoes when reception is quiet.'

'They wanted him special,' Henderson said. 'All those Germans need their boots cleaned.'

'Germans,' the woman said, as she spat on a sheet before folding it. 'I've been having a nice time these last weeks with Paris so quiet. Now they're turning everything upside down. Threw out all our guests, including residents who've lived here for years, then went down to the cellar and dragged up all the best wines and champagne. You can bet they won't be paying their bills and if I don't see my wages I'm out of here.'

'That's the breaks, I guess,' Henderson said uncertainly as he turned towards the door. 'You wouldn't know how I can find out what room Mannstein's in would you? I don't want to go back upstairs and make myself look stupid.'

The woman tutted with contempt, but pointed towards a telephone on the wall. 'Dial zero, zero for the front desk. They'll give you his room number.'

As Henderson grabbed the phone, the laundress

walked over to a clothes rail and grabbed a set of pressed overalls. 'You'd better put them on,' she said. 'If the floor manager catches you in a public area without a uniform he'll go spare.'

Then the woman looked at Marc. 'We've never had a boy shoe-shine before. The only thing I've got that will fit you is a messenger's uniform. But don't go getting polish on it because it'll never come out of white cuffs.'

'Thank you.' Marc nodded to her as he grabbed the hanger. His uniform comprised a white shirt, black trousers and a velvet waistcoat with gold buttons.

'Very fetching,' Henderson teased, as they stepped back into the corridor.

'Did you get the room number from reception?' Marc asked.

'Six-one-two,' Henderson replied. 'Now we need somewhere to put these clothes on.'

They headed back upstairs and passed a janitor's cupboard that was big enough to change in. Henderson closed the door behind them, switched on the light and unzipped the bag, taking out the compact machine gun and showing Marc how to take off the safety catch, fire and reload. On the way out, he grabbed a mop, plunger and bucket.

'Now we've got to find the lift.'

The staff area on the ground floor was a warren and it

took several anxious minutes of wandering badly-lit corridors until they found themselves near the hotel's reception desk with the main elevators facing directly towards them.

Several Gestapo officers were returning to their rooms. The lift stopped at the second and fifth floors and on each the departing officers were saluted by two German infantrymen on guard duty.

'Seems they've got this place sealed up pretty tight,' Henderson said.

They were alone for the final ride to the top floor and Henderson used the opportunity to check that his silenced pistol was ready to fire.

'You sure you're OK with the machine gun?' Henderson said. 'Remember to hold it exactly how I showed you or you'll rip your shoulder off.'

The two guards stepped forwards as the lift doors opened. 'State your purpose,' one guard said, in truly awful French.

Henderson began to mumble a convoluted explanation about blocked pipes in room 612 and how the messenger boy's little arms would be needed to reach behind a sink and undo a valve. Of course, the Germans didn't understand a word.

'Blocked toilet,' the German said irritably. 'That's all you need to tell me.'

Henderson nodded apologetically as he walked off with Marc in tow. But after a few steps he realised he'd gone the wrong way and he turned around. Once they'd passed the guards again, one spoke to the other in German.

'Useless bloody French,' he sneered. 'Too much wine. It's no wonder they lost the bloody war.'

Henderson and Marc both thought it best to pretend that they hadn't understood and carried on towards Mannstein's room. Fortunately there were several turns in the corridor and two sets of fire doors.

'As soon as Mannstein opens the door I'm going to shoot him in the face,' Henderson said. 'Stand well back unless you want to get splattered in blood.'

'Right.' Marc nodded, taking a deep breath as he poised his knuckles in front of the door. Henderson dropped his bucket and mop and pulled the silenced pistol.

Marc knocked and waited.

'Who is it?' a German said.

'Messenger boy,' Marc shouted.

Henderson panicked. 'That's not Mannstein,' he gasped.

Marc didn't have time to ask what to do as a Gestapo officer opened the door. 'Message from Oberst Hinze—' he began.

But before Marc knew it, Henderson had fired his shot and a mist of the officer's blood had spattered his face. Marc was stunned as Henderson burst into the room, just in time to hear Mannstein cry out and run for the bathroom. The bolt slid across the door a second before Henderson barged into it.

'I just want to talk, Mr Mannstein,' Henderson lied. 'It's not too late. I can still get you out of France.'

Inside the bathroom, Mannstein was going frantic. Banging against the wall, stamping on the floor and screaming for help. He wasn't a fool and he knew Henderson wasn't here to talk.

'Machine gun,' Henderson shouted, pointing towards the bag.

Marc handed the gun over and Henderson stepped away from the door and let rip. The bullets shredded the door. Henderson used his fist to punch through a large hole and then aimed directly at Mannstein, who'd taken shelter by lying flat in the bath.

A second blast from the Sten gun turned him into red goo, but Mannstein's cries and the gunfire had been heard by the guards down the corridor and by several Gestapo officers in their rooms.

The first black uniform came out of the room directly across the corridor. Marc dived to the floor as the officer took aim with his pistol, but Henderson spun around and annihilated him with the machine gun.

'Shit,' Henderson howled. 'Shit, shit, shit.'

'Never mind shit,' Marc said, as he grabbed the pistol from the dead German's hand. 'What do we do?'

'What do you think we do?' Henderson said as he charged towards the door. 'Run like hell!'

CHAPTER TWENTY-FIVE

Charles Henderson and Marc Kilgour belted down the corridor. The German guards were out of sight, but could be heard barging through the fire doors behind them.

Marc's greatest fear was a dead end, but the carpeted corridor ended with a door leading on to a fire escape. As they ploughed through, Henderson noticed a fire-alarm handle on the wall and gave it a pull.

'Should set the cat among the pigeons,' Henderson gasped, as they raced down the stairs with the alarm ringing in their ears.

There were two flights between each floor and as they reached the fifth floor a Gestapo officer in a dressing gown was peering down the hallway, wondering if the alarm was for real. Henderson took aim with the machine gun, but the magazine jammed. At the same moment one of the guards above them leaned over the banister and blasted several automatic rounds, tearing chunks of soft plaster out of the wall and shattering a tall window.

Henderson ditched the machine gun and used his silenced pistol to kill the German standing in the doorway. More random shots came from above as the pair made it down to the fourth floor, where a small group of German officers stood on the landing.

'French troops,' Henderson shouted, hiding his pistol as he pointed upwards and tried his best to sound like a panicked maintenance man. 'They've shot two officers and started a fire.'

Marc barged through the crowd with his German pistol tucked inside his trousers. The Germans dived for cover as more bullets rained from above. One daring officer decided to go upstairs and investigate. He was machine-gunned by a green-uniformed guard coming the other way before he made it up three steps.

All Marc could hear as he made it to the third floor was a lot of swearing and yelling in German. Men were filing out on to the staircase, some heading up to investigate the shots and screams up on the next landing, some evacuating because of the fire alarm and the remainder milling about looking as if they needed someone to give them orders.

Henderson reckoned the staircase would become dangerous when the Germans stopped arguing and worked out who they were really after, so he led Marc through the double doors and into a corridor identical to the one they'd evacuated three storeys further up.

'Don't run,' Henderson said, as he slowed to a brisk walk.

Because of their hotel uniforms, the Germans they passed in the hallway accepted their presence and some even looked to them for advice.

'Probably just a false alarm, sir,' Henderson explained, sticking to French because it might be suspicious if he used his near perfect German. 'Go downstairs to the lobby and the fire marshals will direct you out of the building.'

Once they'd passed a dozen rooms and two sets of swinging doors, Marc reckoned they were relatively safe.

'Chaos is the best disguise of all,' Henderson said.

Immediately ahead of them, a door clicked open and a young Gestapo officer emerged from his room, buttoning his tunic. His movements were calm and he clearly assumed that the fire alarm was fake.

'What's happening here, gentlemen?' the officer asked.

Marc expected Henderson to politely tell the officer that he didn't know and point him towards the fire escape, but before he knew what was going on, the German officer was backing into his room with Henderson's silenced pistol aimed at his head.

'Get in here, shut the door,' Henderson ordered.

Marc rushed into the plush hotel room and shut the door as Henderson forced the Gestapo officer to sit down on the bed.

'Strip,' Henderson ordered, before turning towards Marc. 'Where's your pistol?'

'Tucked in here,' the boy said, as he pulled it out of his trousers.

'I'm going to put on his uniform,' Henderson explained. 'Keep your gun aimed at the Boche while I change. If he makes a move, shoot him in the head.'

Henderson rested his gun on a wooden chest as he unbuttoned his overall. Marc stood with his gun aimed at the German, who didn't seem to be in any rush to undress.

'You'll both end up before a firing squad,' the young officer said, as he unbuttoned his shirt.

'Maybe,' Henderson said curtly. 'But you'll be dead a bloody sight sooner than that if you don't get a move on.'

The gun felt heavy and Marc was alarmed as the officer dropped his trousers, revealing a jock-strap and a leather sheath containing an ivory-handled dagger set with a gold swastika. Henderson could see the tension in Marc's face and tried to reassure him.

'Don't you worry,' Henderson said. 'If he's in the Gestapo, he's bright enough to know that a bullet travels faster than a knife.'

Once the two men were both stripped down to underwear, Henderson took his silenced pistol and ruthlessly shot the German through the head. A great red splat hit the wall behind the bed and a chunk of hair and skull slid down the wall. Marc was so shocked that he stumbled back towards the door and almost dropped his gun.

'Bloody hell,' the boy gasped. 'Couldn't you have tied him up, or knocked him out?'

Henderson shook his head as he stepped into the dead officer's black trousers. 'Tying up takes for ever and knocking out is an imprecise science at best. If you stick a bullet through his brain, you know he won't be coming back at you.'

Marc could understand the logic, but the ruthless act had dented his faith. Henderson had seemed different back at the house when he'd given Marc water and cleaned his face, but was he really just as bad as Oberst Hinze?

'Don't just stand there,' Henderson snapped, as he

pointed towards a battered suitcase lying on the floor. 'See what you can get. That's a German pistol you're holding and he might have spare ammunition.'

As well as two clips and a box of ammo, Marc found three grenades on a belt, wrapped inside a set of battle fatigues that stank of urine and sweat.

'Are these any use?' Marc asked.

Henderson broke into a broad smile. 'The ability to blow stuff up is always useful,' he said, nodding. 'So what do you think of the uniform? It's not perfect, but I think I can pull it off.'

Marc nodded. 'He was a bit taller than you, but it's OK.'

'I'd lose the velvet jacket,' Henderson said. 'It's distinctive and they might be looking for it.'

'So what's our plan?' Marc asked, as he took off the waistcoat. 'Or are you still working on it?'

Henderson looked at the striped markings on his black uniform as he placed a grey, peaked cap on his head. 'Looks like our friend Mr Corpse was a senior officer. Nobody will expect us to head out the front of the hotel and get in a German car, so that's exactly what we'll do.'

Marc looked aghast. 'Are you insane?'

'We've caused panic,' Henderson said, as he stared into the mirror and looked at his stubble. He didn't quite look the part, but there was no time to shave. 'Once the panic dies down they'll lock this hotel down tighter than the Führer's toupee.'

With that, Henderson placed his silenced pistol into a leather holster and passed one of the grenades to Marc.

'Once you pull the pin, you've got about fifteen seconds before it explodes.'

'OK,' Marc said weakly, as he stared briefly at the grenade before forcing it into his trousers.

With a gun tucked into the waistline and a grenade bulging from his pocket, Marc worried that his trousers were going to fall down as he left the hotel room and followed Henderson's black uniform down the corridor.

The fire alarm meant the lifts were out of action, so they walked down the staircase that ran beside it. The alarm itself had stopped ringing, but the plush lobby was crammed with confused Gestapo officers. Nobody paid the blindest bit of notice as Marc and Henderson shuffled between bodies.

Marc caught snippets of conversation. Depending upon who you listened to the situation varied from French commandos holding men hostage on the top floor, to a fire, to a hoax played by a drunken officer.

'Coming through,' Henderson said, speaking his most pompous German and holding Marc firmly by the shoulder. 'Urgent message from the Oberst.'

As Henderson approached the doors at the front of the lobby he pulled the pin from the grenade and dropped it into the earth beneath a potted palm. Marc had never been through a revolving door and looked perplexed, but it wasn't the right moment to hang around and Henderson gave him an almighty shove before shuffling around inside the door. They stepped out into fresh air and a line of officers smoking and holding glasses of wine. It was almost nine and the sky was purple.

'Excuse me, gentlemen,' Henderson said, as he pushed Marc through the line of officers. 'I must escort this messenger.'

As soon as Henderson broke clear of the officers and started down the steps a German infantryman who looked no more than eighteen stood in front of Henderson, clicked his heels and gave a Nazi salute.

'Heil Hitler. Do you require transport, sir?'

Henderson was counting in his head and knew that the grenade would explode within four seconds. 'Something fast,' he said, pointing towards a motorcycle with a sidecar. 'Are the keys in the ignition?'

'Yes, Herr Major,' the infantryman said, nodding. 'Fully fuelled and ready to—'

A white flash erupted from the front of the hotel, followed by a shower of glass and smoke that sent a dozen Gestapo officers toppling down the hotel's front steps. Screams rang from inside as Henderson grabbed Marc and dragged him towards the motorbike.

Henderson felt a sharp pain where a splinter of glass had nicked his ear, but he had to ignore it as he straddled the bike and Marc vaulted into the sidecar. Henderson kicked the starter and he felt the engine vibrate between his legs, but he hardly heard a thing because his ears still rang from the blast.

'When I stop, you run to the car and grab the bag from the trunk,' he shouted.

Marc wasn't sure what Henderson meant, but realised once he'd taken a sharp left out of the hotel driveway and another into the side street where he'd parked his battered Fiat. The boy had one leg out of the sidecar before they stopped at the kerb.

Henderson kept the motorbike running as Marc struggled to open the trunk.

'Push the button and twist the handle,' Henderson shouted, as a set of headlights turned into the alleyway behind them.

It only took Marc a few seconds to get into the back of the Fiat, but it felt like minutes. He grabbed Henderson's briefcase – which contained gold and money – and his own pigskin bag and threw them into the sidecar before jumping on top of them.

Henderson realised that the Mercedes saloon behind them was driving too fast to be routine traffic. It was coming after them, with a brace of motorcycles for company.

'Use your pistol,' Henderson ordered. 'See if you can fend some of them off.'

He pulled away from the kerb while Marc was still perched awkwardly on top of the briefcase.

CHAPTER TWENTY-SIX

Age had shrivelled Yvette Doran, but years of farm work had kept her fit and her movements were swift and precise. Each night she made Hugo and Paul share a tin bath and inspected them for cleanliness afterwards.

'Nails,' she said firmly, as the two boys stood in front of her wearing pyjama bottoms donated by a neighbour.

Hugo held out his hands and Yvette brushed her calloused thumb across the youngster's soft skin. It had been many years since the old lady had looked after kids and the podgy softness of the six year old's hands made her smile.

'Not bad,' she said fondly, as she kissed Hugo on the forehead. 'And you combed your hair so it doesn't tangle. Now show me those teeth.'

Hugo opened up proudly.

'I'll make a gentleman out of you yet,' she said. 'But you need to get around the back more with the toothbrush. Don't just clean at the front.'

Hugo leaned forwards and gave Yvette a kiss on the cheek. 'Goodnight,' he said fondly, before bouncing up the wooden staircase on his bare feet.

Paul was five years older and the old lady took a quick glance at his nails and made him lean forwards to check behind his ears.

'How come you don't do this to Rosie?' Paul asked.

Yvette laughed. 'She's almost a woman. I don't trust you boys.'

At first Paul had found the inspection a little embarrassing, but he knew that the old lady had a good heart and a week had been enough to get used to her eccentricities.

'I'll miss you and your sister when you go,' Yvette said.

'We'll write to you from England,' Paul said brightly, but the prospect of leaving made him sad. The Dorans' cottage was a comfortable refuge from the war and much as he wanted to fulfil his father's wishes and return to Britain with Mannstein's documents, he wasn't relishing the prospect of more refugee-strewn roads and a potentially dangerous sea voyage.

'You can stay down here and draw for an hour if you

want before bedtime,' the old lady said.

Paul shook his head. 'I'll just say goodnight to the Father, then I'll go upstairs and help Rosie pack.'

He walked from the kitchen to the living room, but found the retired priest asleep in his armchair with a newspaper strewn over his lap and reading glasses balanced on the tip of his nose. Paul didn't want to disturb him, so he crept upstairs and found Rosie. Strands of wet hair hung down her nightdress as she arranged clean clothes inside a suitcase. Hugo always seemed to find a second wind around bedtime and he was jumping energetically on the bed.

'How's it going, sis?' Paul asked, as he broke into a yawn.

Rosie shrugged. 'Not too bad. Henderson said he was coming by car, so we should be able to carry everything we want.'

'That's good,' Paul said, as Hugo did the splits and crashed off the end of the bed, hitting the floor with a thud.

Rosie rushed over to pick him up. 'I told you that would happen if you went crazy,' she said pointedly.

The youngster had banged his knee quite badly, but he didn't want to admit that Rosie was right so he fought off the urge to sob.

'All right, bossy-boots,' Hugo groaned, as he dived face

first on to his bed of old sofa cushions. 'You're no fun!'

'You're like a rubber ball,' Paul grinned. 'We could drop you from the top of the stairs and you'd probably bounce.'

'Why have you two got to go?' Hugo asked seriously, as he rolled on to his back and brought his leg up to inspect a graze on his knee.

Rosie had explained already, and whilst she liked Hugo, he did tend to get on your nerves by the end of the day. '*Because,*' she said firmly. 'Now go to sleep.'

'But why go?' Hugo moaned. 'I'll have no one to play with.'

'Hugo,' Paul said firmly. 'Everyone belongs somewhere. We belong in England. When your daddy comes back from being a soldier, you'll belong with him.'

'I don't want *him* back,' Hugo said, looking thoroughly disgusted. 'I can come on the boat with you.'

'But what about Yvette and Father Doran?' Rosie said, as she closed her suitcase. 'You like them and you like running around in the fields. And there are other boys in the village you can play with.'

'I hate those boys,' Hugo said.

Paul laughed. 'How do you know that? You've never even met them.'

'They're smelly,' Hugo insisted. 'I like you two better.'

Rosie sensed that Hugo was going to end up crying

and decided to change the subject. 'I tell you what,' she said. 'It's probably going to be our last night together, so why don't you cuddle up with us?'

The six year old didn't need a second invitation and he dived under the blankets at the bottom of the bed and then wriggled beneath the covers until his head emerged between the pillows at the top. Paul and Rosie smiled at each other, both wishing they were still young enough to get their kicks so easily.

Rosie turned to her brother as Hugo messed with the pillows. 'I'm sorry about earlier,' she said awkwardly. 'I shouldn't have ripped your drawing. You must have spent hours on that.'

'I guess it *was* pretty sick,' Paul said. 'And sorry I called you fat. You're not – obviously.'

Rosie laughed. 'Remember when Dad used to tease me and say that I had good child-bearing hips?'

'You used to go bananas,' Paul said, smiling, before mocking his sister's voice: '*I'm not ever getting married. I'm not ever having horrible babies.*'

'So are you OK about tomorrow?' Rosie asked when they'd finished laughing. 'Or whenever Mr Henderson gets here.'

'Kind of,' Paul said. 'Dad trusted him, so I reckon he'll be OK.'

'I wonder about later on,' Rosie admitted. 'I mean,

Mum didn't have anyone over here and Dad's only got those weird second cousins up in Yorkshire.'

'Freaks.' Paul nodded. 'Their kids practically had strings of drool hanging out of their mouths. But Dad had some money and Granddad's old house in London. We'll probably get sent to boarding schools and live there in the holidays.'

'Mum never wanted us to board,' Rosie said. 'She said they're really strict. Too many canings and stuff.'

'You'll be OK,' Paul said uncertainly. 'Nobody gives you any hassle. But I'm skinny and I bet they'll make me play rugby . . .'

'We're thinking too hard,' Rosie said, as she tried not to smirk at the prospect of Paul getting crunched in a rugby scrum. 'We're not even out of France yet. Maybe with the war we won't even have to go to school.'

'Are you two coming into bed or not?' Hugo demanded.

'Yeah, we're coming,' Rosie said. It was early and worrying about leaving meant she probably wouldn't get to sleep for hours. But she'd miss Hugo and wanted to cuddle up and watch him fall asleep.

Paul flicked off the light switch and the siblings walked barefoot in the dark, ending up on opposite sides of the bed with Hugo sandwiched between them. Hugo nuzzled Rosie's chest and slid his arm around her back.

'Goodnight,' Rosie said gently, but she smelled something as she closed her eyes and took a breath.

'Christ!' Paul moaned. 'Who farted?'

Hugo broke into hysterics as Rosie kicked off the blankets. 'That's unbearable,' she choked. 'How can someone so little make a smell that bad?'

Paul grabbed the pillow beneath his head and used it to whack Hugo over the head.

'Smell my fart,' Hugo chanted, as he took Rosie's pillow and swung back at Paul. 'Smell my fart, smell my fart, smell my fart!'

Rosie jumped out of bed and couldn't help smiling as she watched the two outlines rumbling in the dark. She thought about turning on the light and breaking them up, but she didn't feel like being sensible, so she grabbed the pillow from Hugo's bed and dived into the action.

CHAPTER TWENTY-SEVEN

Most of the German firepower that entered Paris earlier in the day had exited south, where it was being used to press the Germans' advantage over the retreating French. Paris was a ghost town. Every shop closed, every road empty. There were no checkpoints and few patrols, but the Germans' fearsome reputation kept the population indoors. Marc, Henderson and the pursuing Germans seemed to have the streets of Paris to themselves.

Henderson clipped a kerb as they rounded a tight corner. Marc found himself half a metre off the ground in the sidecar as Henderson threw his weight to correct the tilt whilst struggling to avoid a line of dustbins.

The Mercedes had a higher top speed than the bike and sidecar, but that counted for little on the tight streets of Paris. The driver never got close enough for the passenger to open fire and after three corners it had dropped out of sight. The two pursuing motorbikes were nimbler and as they didn't have the weight of a sidecar they were also faster than their prey.

But the Germans couldn't make their speed count because Marc lay on his belly in the sidecar and shot at them whenever they closed in. And what the bikes gained in a straight line, Henderson pulled back on hilltops and blind corners. He'd lived in Paris for years and knew the streets, whereas the Germans had to slow down because they didn't know what lay ahead.

By the time Henderson had got all three wheels back on the ground, the German riders pursuing them were the closest they'd been. Marc's first shots had been crazy, but he was getting the hang of the pistol and had already hit one of the bikes, although the shot had deflected off the front wheel arch.

Henderson slowed down to turn right and suddenly the headlamp on the lead bike was right in Marc's face, less than four metres away. He pulled the trigger and hit the rider square in the chest. The shot knocked the man backwards as they turned the corner. Marc was astonished to see the motorbike continue in a straight line, whilst its rider froze in midair, legs apart and hands out front as though he was still riding.

'I got one,' Marc yelled.

Henderson couldn't acknowledge this because they'd turned on to a steeply descending street paved with cobbles. The homes built close to the kerb on either side passed in a blur. They were gaining speed, but Henderson knew that the sidecar didn't have its own brake and if he tried to slow its momentum would pull them into a hopeless spin.

Marc's shoulder banged against the sidecar as he saw the single headlight of the remaining bike poised at the top of the hill. But it wasn't coming after them.

'I think he's chickened out!' Marc shouted jubilantly.

Henderson was closing on the bottom of the hill and there was a tight turn just ahead. If they didn't make it, he was going to crash into a metal fence before careering over the handlebars and slamming head first into a wall without a crash helmet.

He waited until the hill started to level before dabbing the brakes, but there was still enough force to send Marc sliding down inside the body of the sidecar. Each time the sidecar tried to outrun the motorbike to which it was joined, it pitched to one side. Henderson would correct this by steering in the opposite direction and Marc would hit the metal with a thud. The process was repeated each time Henderson applied the brake and, as if the buffeting inside the sidecar wasn't enough, Marc managed to bang his face on the briefcase, tearing off the blood clot around his missing tooth.

More by luck than judgement, Henderson slowed down enough to steer around the sharp corner without even brushing the kerb. Marc pushed his feet against the bottom of the footwell and clutched his bloody chin as he manoeuvred himself back into the seat cushion facing forwards.

'Have they gone?' Henderson asked breathlessly, as he took a quick right into a side street, followed by a left on to a much gentler hill.

'I shot one,' Marc explained, as his tongue fought the blood in his mouth. 'The other obviously didn't fancy his chances.'

Henderson looked pleased and he eased off the throttle until the bike was cruising. It was heaps quieter than when they'd been going flat out.

'Have you got something to wipe your mouth?' Henderson asked.

'Just looking,' Marc said, as he reached into the pigskin bag and found the square of cloth in which he'd originally wrapped Director Tomas' food. He wiped his face before rolling up a corner of the cloth. Then he pushed it into the gap where his tooth had been and bit down to try and stop the bleeding.

Henderson pulled on to a wide boulevard. Marc

looked around and realised that they were near the centre of Paris, in the Government quarter. The tall building on one side of the road had burned out in an air raid and moonlight shone through a stone façade with nothing but air behind the shattered windows.

'You did great,' Henderson said. 'The one you shot, do you reckon you killed him?'

'Maybe,' Marc said uncertainly. 'It was like he stopped moving and the bike carried on.'

'Are you OK about it?'

Marc nodded. 'You think I care about Germans after Hinze ripped my tooth out? So what now?'

'Potente has four or five hours' advantage over us and he'll have an easier time getting through the German lines than I would.'

'So why didn't we go straight after him?' Marc asked.

Henderson looked uncomfortable. 'I would have liked to for the sake of Digby Clarke's kids, but Mannstein was more important. He could have recreated his plans within weeks and the Germans would have shipped him off to Poland before I could possibly get back from Tours.'

'So if we can't get to Tours before Potente we're stuffed?'

'Not necessarily,' Henderson said. 'We'll have to pray that some of the phone lines out of Paris are still working. If they are, we might be able to get a message down there.'

Marc looked surprised. 'But I don't even know the name of the person they're staying with, let alone the phone number.'

'I know,' Henderson said, nodding. 'But you said they were staying with a retired priest on a farm south of Tours. That might be enough – for the sakes of Paul and Rosie Clarke, it had better be.'

'So if we're not going to Tours, where are we going?'

'There's a telephone exchange just a few hundred metres from here. They'll have phone and street directories for the whole of France. We need to get in there, but it's likely to be under guard to prevent saboteurs.'

'Sounds great,' Marc said, as a drop of blood trickled from his chin on to his white shirt.

CHAPTER TWENTY-EIGHT

Marc hunkered in the footwell of the sidecar as Henderson rolled up outside an office building. The carved wooden door had a brass plaque bearing the logo of France Télécom. A single German infantryman guarded the door, but he only seemed interested in the finger jammed up his nose and he was stunned by the sight of Henderson in Gestapo uniform. He bolted to attention and gave an anxious salute.

'Heil Hitler,' Henderson said, as he accepted the salute with a flick of his wrist. 'I have orders from Oberst Hinze to access the directories and switchboard inside this telephone exchange.'

The infantryman nodded. 'Very good, Herr Major. One of our engineers is working inside and should be able to assist you.'

'Boy,' Henderson shouted, as he looked back towards the sidecar.

Marc sat up. 'Please don't hit me again, sir,' he said meekly.

The guard was shocked by the sobbing boy with blood pouring down his chin, but it only served to enhance his opinion of the Gestapo. Regular German troops feared the black uniforms almost as much as the civilians in the countries they occupied. So while the baby-faced guard found the situation odd, he had no intention of quizzing a Gestapo officer.

The inside of the exchange was stuffy, with the smell of sparks and oil in the air. Henderson led Marc across a reception area and under an archway to a dim space lined with racks containing thousands of mechanical switches. Over a third of Paris's telephone traffic went through this exchange, with each call connected by the shuddering racks of gears and cogs.

'Heil Hitler,' a bespectacled German said, when he saw Henderson. 'What can I do for you, Major?'

'Are the telephone lines working?' Henderson asked bluntly.

'We're having difficulty. Many staff didn't come to work because of the curfew,' he explained. 'We only have four French operators out of more than sixty. Calls within the city work through the automated exchange, but long-distance calls require manual connection. The operators can't cope, so I've restricted long-distance calling to military traffic.'

'I need a connection to Tours,' Henderson explained. 'Is that possible?'

'I'll speak to one of the operators. We have connected some calls to Southern France successfully, but the network is very busy. It can take a long time and some local operators are disconnecting anyone they overhear speaking in German.'

'My French is good,' Henderson said. 'Tell the operator to start making a connection to Tours immediately.'

'Yes, Herr Major,' the engineer said, before striding purposefully towards a woman at a manual switchboard.

Henderson stepped over to a metal shelf and grabbed the two bulky directories that contained every telephone number in France. He flipped quickly through the pages until he found the listing for Tours. The town had more than 100,000 inhabitants, but less than 2,000 had telephones.

Henderson turned to Marc as he pulled a fountain pen from his uniform and unscrewed the cap. He looked around to make sure the engineer was out of hearing before speaking in a whisper. 'Can you read and write?'

'Course I bloody can,' Marc said indignantly.

'You scan the right-hand page, I'll take the left. I want you to take out any phone number that's for a church or a religious organisation. Or anyone listed as a priest or a minister.'

'But how will we know which one?'

Henderson shook his head. 'We won't. But priests, rabbis and other ministers within a community usually know one another. If we can get a couple of calls through, the chances are they'll know about the retired priest who took in two children and be able to pass on a warning message. Even if they don't know him, they'll know of someone who does.'

'That makes sense,' Marc said, nodding. 'But aren't priests too poor to have telephones?'

'That could be a problem,' Henderson acknowledged. 'But we only need one man, even if it's the Bishop of Tours himself.'

The pair began running their fingers down the listing of Tours telephone numbers. Each page took a minute to scan and when they'd both finished, Henderson would flip over to the next.

After four pages the German engineer approached. He pointed to the pretty operator seated at a switchboard twenty metres away. 'Marte is trying to establish a connection. She rates our chances of getting through at about fifty-fifty.'

'Thank you,' Henderson said, curtly. 'I'll call if I need you again.'

Their eyes were straining by the time they got through the last page of listings, but they'd ended up with three numbers that looked hopeful and Henderson jotted them down before replacing the directory on its shelf and stepping up to the operator. She didn't look comfortable with the black uniform and Marc's bloody face.

'How are we doing?' Henderson asked, in French.

'It's difficult,' Marte explained, as she pointed to her tall console filled with connection sockets and dangling wires. 'Normally, a connection to Tours requires only two links, via the exchanges in Le Mans and Tours. But Le Mans was damaged in a Boche air raid last night and . . .'

The word Boche was offensive to Germans and Marte turned white as she looked around at Henderson. 'I mean . . . a *German* air raid, sir. Now we have to route calls to Tours via Dijon, Lyon and Bourges. With the network so busy and many lines damaged by bombing it can take a very long time to contact the various operators and establish a long-distance connection.'

'I see,' Henderson said. 'Where are we now?'

'I'm waiting for the operator in Dijon. She'll contact me as soon as she has a line available to Tours.'

'Can you tell them it's important?' Henderson said.

Marte shook her head. 'They know Paris is occupied and there's a risk they'll cut us off. Operators in some towns have stopped connecting our traffic.'

Marc and Henderson waited while the operator continued her business, answering calls and moving wires across her console from one plug to another. Henderson was nervous. He had no idea how good the Germans' radio communications were, but it could only be a matter of time before every soldier in Paris was on the lookout for a man and boy who'd stolen a Gestapo uniform and a motorbike with sidecar.

After fifteen anxious minutes, a white light flashed above the word *Dijon* on the console. The operator plugged in a jack and picked up her handset.

'I see,' she said sadly. 'Thank you for trying, Elène.'

The operator turned towards Henderson. 'I'm sorry, Major. The operator in Dijon says she can't find a line.'

Henderson looked around to make sure that the German engineer was out of sight. 'I'm not really Gestapo,' he confessed. 'I'm a British agent and we need to get out of here before we're caught. If I left you a message, is there any way that you might try again later and pass it to one of these numbers in Tours? The lives of two children are in danger.'

The operator looked sceptical, suspecting that this was a Gestapo trick to test her loyalty. She spoke in broken

English. 'If you are an Englishman, I assume you can understand what I am saying?'

Henderson smiled, before whispering his answer in English. 'English is my native tongue. And if you study the hem of my trousers, you'll see that this uniform is tailored for a fellow somewhat taller than myself.'

The operator's English wasn't good enough to understand all of this, but she understood the body language and glanced down at his hem. Then Henderson opened his tunic to reveal that his waistband was too big to do up his trousers properly.

'You must have some nerve,' Marte said, as she cracked a nervous smile. 'I can take your message and pass it through to these numbers, or if you can wait two or three minutes I can connect you with Tours.'

Henderson's jaw dropped. 'Three minutes!'

'I'll work for the Boche,' Marte said mischievously. 'But that doesn't mean that I'll make it easy for them.'

She plugged a jack into the socket marked *Dijon* and grabbed her handset. 'Elène,' she said brightly. 'I've got one for France. I need the Tours exchange quickly.'

It seemed that when a call was for France phone lines opened up with miraculous speed. Apart from half a minute waiting for the operator in Bourges to answer, the connection to Tours was made and a telephone rang three hundred kilometres away. Unfortunately, nobody picked up.

'Try another,' Henderson said anxiously.

With the connection from Paris established, it was a simple matter for the operator in Tours to dial another number. This time it was a parochial house and the phone was answered by a young priest named Father Fry.

Fry said he didn't know of the retired priest, but that one of his older housemates almost certainly would. The young priest gave his word to pass on the message to wherever the retired priest happened to be, even if it meant walking there himself.

'Bless you, Father,' Henderson said brightly. 'And tell them that I'm heading south, but it may take me a day or two to reach them.'

Henderson returned the handset to the operator when the call ended. 'Try the third number,' he said. 'Father Fry sounded reliable, but I'd rather be safe than sorry.'

After a couple of minutes, a call came through. Marte shook her head as she put down the receiver.

'No connection,' she explained. 'The Tours operator said that the number was for a Catholic college in the city centre and that there was a lot of bomb damage around there.'

Henderson shrugged. 'Pity,' he said. 'I just hope we can rely on Father Fry.'

'What now?' Marc asked.

'I'm exhausted,' Henderson answered. 'I need a night's sleep, then I'll set off for Tours in the morning.'

Marc looked unsettled. 'You're not going to abandon me are you?'

'I suppose not,' Henderson said uncertainly.

'Have you got anywhere we can stay?' Marc asked.

'Not near here, but I have keys for the apartment where my assistant used to live. It's a twenty-minute ride.' Henderson turned towards the operator. 'Thank you so much for your help.'

Marte smiled. 'Rule Britannia,' she whispered.

'*Vive la France*,' Henderson replied. Then he checked that the engineer was out of sight before kissing her on both cheeks.

CHAPTER TWENTY-NINE

The Government hadn't surrendered, but giving up Paris without destroying tactically important bridges across the Seine showed that they'd abandoned any realistic hope of defending the rest of France. Soldiers were deserting or surrendering en masse and the roads south were lined with troops. Tired and hungry, they faced walks of hundreds of kilometres to get home.

Herr Potente passed thousands of these disarmed Frenchmen as he drove towards Tours in an Austin motorcar that had been commandeered and refuelled by the Gestapo. Unlike the civilian refugees the Clarke family had encountered a week earlier, the soldiers had no carts or prams to block the road and all but a few hopeless drunks stuck close to the kerb.

Craters, fallen brickwork and demolished bridges were Potente's main concerns. Most required simple detours through villages or farm tracks but in places crossing a river meant diversions of up to thirty kilometres and nerve-wracking rides across bridges held in place by mounded rubble and hastily wedged railway sleepers.

Potente was immensely unhappy at the way his day had turned out. He worked for the Abwehr, a branch of German military intelligence that was engaged in a power struggle with the Gestapo. Potente considered himself a professional spy; while the Gestapo were agents of the Nazi party, and he thought them little better than organised thugs.

Being openly criticised by Oberst Hinze annoyed Potente. His team of six agents had operated in Paris since before the invasion and they'd successfully unearthed thirty British agents, killing eight and forcing the rest to flee ahead of the invasion.

At least Potente hoped to be out of France soon. The Russians were German allies, France would surrender soon and Potente could see no option for Britain other than to sign a peace treaty with Hitler. With luck, the war would be over soon and he planned to return to his family home near Hamburg and see out his remaining years in peace.

*

Potente reached Tours shortly after sun-up and stopped to eat croissants he'd brought from Paris and drink tepid coffee from a vacuum flask. He was tired from driving through the night and hoped the coffee would give him a kick-start to get through the day.

He anticipated no problems with picking up the plans and the children, but the call from Rosie Clarke seemed to have come at a remarkably convenient moment and, like any spy, he was always wary of a trap.

After eating, he opened his revolver to check that it was fully loaded before spinning the barrel and snapping it shut with a flick of the wrist. Potente was fond of this sound and couldn't resist repeating the action several times.

He checked his map and guessed that Father Doran's cottage would be a quarter-hour's drive, but the petrol gauge was close to empty so he took a can and a funnel from the trunk and refuelled before setting off.

The Dorans' cottage wasn't dissimilar to the one Herr Potente had lived in as a boy. He felt a twinge of rural nostalgia as he pulled on a frayed cord to ring the bell above the front door. Yvette Doran wandered up the driveway from behind him, carrying a shovel and wearing boots covered in mud.

'Mr Henderson?' Yvette said uncertainly, before cracking a warm smile. 'I didn't expect you so early.'

Potente spoke in perfect French. 'I made good time. The roads are surprisingly quiet.'

Yvette nodded. 'I think everyone has been moving around France for so long that they've finally given up. Do step inside. The door isn't locked and I expect my brother is dealing with the children's breakfast.'

The door creaked as it opened directly into a living room. The way through to the kitchen was clear and Potente noted the three children sitting at the dining table. He correctly assumed that Paul and Rosie were the two older ones.

'Welcome, Mr Henderson,' Father Doran said, as he stood up to move towards the stove. 'You've had a long journey. Would you like some fresh coffee?'

'Wonderful,' Potente said, smelling the bread baking in the oven as he rubbed his hands and looked at the children. 'I'm afraid we can't stay for long. I got a Morse-code signal through to London and I've secured us a place on a ship from Bordeaux, but it's leaving at thirteen-hundred, which is cutting things a little fine.'

'We've heard so much about you, Mr Henderson,' Rosie said brightly. 'Our father often spoke about you.'

'Really?' Potente said warily.

Father Doran placed a mug of coffee on the dining table. 'Do sit down, Mr Henderson.'

Paul looked up as Potente took a chair. 'You and

my father were on the same ship for a while, weren't you?' he asked.

'HMS *Manchester*,' Rosie added.

Potente nodded. 'It was a long time ago, but I'll tell you some stories once we get going. Your father was a great man.'

Hugo chose this moment to push his chair back and get down from the table. The six year old was stunned by the sight of Yvette leaning into the doorway and aiming the barrels of a shotgun at Potente's head. The youngster's expression was enough to make Potente swivel around just as Yvette pulled the trigger.

The blast sent a shower of pellets into Potente's back and shoulder, but shotgun pellets are less deadly than weapons that fire a single projectile and Potente grabbed his revolver as the old lady reloaded.

'Our dad never served on the *Manchester*,' Paul shouted, as he scrambled away from the table.

Yvette took a step closer as she pulled the trigger again. This time the pellets were spread over a tighter area and tore a huge hole in Potente's back. As the German's head hit the dining table, Father Doran was the first to realise that there had been two shots at the same moment.

Hugo slammed into the kitchen dresser as a bullet hit him in the armpit. The projectile kept going, passing through the soft tissue of his lung and shredding his ribcage as it exited through the front of his chest.

'Hugo,' Rosie screamed, as the boy collapsed in front of the cabinet.

Hugo tried to scream as Yvette dropped the shotgun and ran towards him, but blood was flooding his lungs and all he could do was heave the warm liquid into his mouth. Paul couldn't bear to look and he grabbed the back door and stumbled outside, on to crumbled earth with chicken coops on either side of him.

Potente crashed off the dining chair as Rosie snatched the revolver from his dead fingertips.

'Oh Hugo, I'm sorry,' Yvette sobbed, as Father Doran stepped one way then another, unsure what to do. 'We should have kept you out of the way, but . . . I'm so sorry.'

Paul peeked back around the door and watched as the old lady took Hugo's limp body and drew him into a bloody hug. It seemed impossible that the little lad who'd been filling his cheeks with bread and pulling faces across the table two minutes earlier was dead.

CHAPTER THIRTY

Marc hardly slept because of the pain in his mouth, but Henderson had been on his feet for days. He crashed out on Miss McAfferty's bed and slept like the dead. When it got light Marc found tinned fruit and English baked beans in a cupboard. He'd now mastered using a tin opener and once the cans were open he mashed the contents because he was too sore to chew.

He tried the radio, but the apartment hadn't been occupied for two months and the battery was flat. It was undeniably a lady's apartment, with flowery wallpaper and a smell like talcum powder and cats.

'It's almost lunchtime,' Henderson complained, scratching his arse as he wandered into the living room. 'Why didn't you wake me?'

Marc sat in an armchair flicking through a bird spotters' manual.

'I did wonder, but I thought you'd probably shout at me.'

'I might have done,' Henderson said with a smile. 'I've popped a dozen Benzedrine pills to stay awake over the last week. My head's banging like a drum.'

'Makes two of us,' Marc said, baring his lips to show Henderson the bloody sore inside his mouth.

'Did you gargle saltwater like I told you last night? You don't want to get an infection.'

'Three times,' Marc said, nodding. 'So is there a plan for today or are we winging it again?'

'Bit of both, I expect,' Henderson said, rubbing his eyes with his palms before stretching into a yawn. 'I know where I've got to go, but I'm not a hundred per cent on the details. Have you eaten?'

'Just some tinned stuff. There's loads in the cupboard.'

'I'll eat something, then we'll get going. Have you had any thoughts about your plans?'

Marc sounded surprised. 'I'm sticking with you aren't I? I mean . . . if that's OK.'

'I meant longer term. Assuming our message got to the retired priest before Herr Potente, I should be picking up Digby Clarke's kids and catching the boat to England. You don't have any documents, but I can probably pull some strings and get you on board too.'

Marc smiled. 'Really?'

'You were at my side when it counted in the hotel. I'm not sure what my superiors will say when I bring home a stray, but they've never liked me much anyway and once you're on the boat they can hardly send you back.'

Marc was happy enough with this. Making friends and moving to Britain was more than he'd dared hope for when he ran away from the orphanage.

They'd pushed the motorbike into a canal the previous night and once he'd eaten, Henderson decided against wearing the Gestapo uniform. He'd been able to bluff his way past a teenaged soldier to get inside the telephone exchange, but he didn't have the paperwork to make it through a security checkpoint in daylight.

Henderson abandoned his usual smart clothing and dressed like a peasant. He ended up looking like Marc, in working boots, corduroy trousers held up with braces, a white shirt and a broad-rimmed hat to keep the bright sun out of his face.

At first glance they were a father and son; peasants seeking refuge with relatives in the south. Unlike peasants though, Henderson had a silenced pistol in a holster strapped to his chest and his suitcase contained pills, poisons, two grenades and fifteen ingots of twenty-four carat gold. Marc walked with his pigskin bag over his back and a case filled with a light load of clothing and a few tins of food.

The pair walked through Paris' southern suburbs at a brisk pace. It was tiring in the heat, but Marc didn't mind because aching legs took his mind off the dull pain in his mouth. Every so often, they were passed by Germans in Kübelwagens or riding horseback, but the shock of the previous day had worn off and Paris was returning to an uneasy normality. It was a Saturday and children chased through the streets or stood in line at the cinema, while their mothers joined grimmer lines and waited for eggs, milk and bread.

It took an hour to reach the city limits, but the main road south towards Tours was blocked by a German checkpoint. A French car had been parked across one lane and its tyres sliced to stop it from being easily moved away. The open lane was guarded by six German troops who waved military traffic through while turning away civilian vehicles or anyone on foot.

'Don't stare at the checkpoint,' Henderson said sharply, as he tugged Marc across the road and towards a small corner café. 'It looks suspicious.'

Marc glanced around to make sure nobody was in earshot. 'We could go cross country,' he said quietly. 'It looks pretty rural and surely they can't guard every single field.'

'That's true,' Henderson agreed. 'But I want to get to Tours in a day or two at most. If we're forced to walk it will take a lot longer than that.'

'So what do we do?'

'We watch and learn,' Henderson said quietly, as they stepped between the lines of empty tables outside the café.

'I have no bread,' the owner said apologetically, the instant they stepped inside. 'Just coffee and a few scraps I made into soup.'

Henderson was content with black coffee, while Marc asked for the soup and regretted it because it was made mostly with potato and bitter-tasting sausage that left a skin of grease on the surface. They lingered for an hour, saying very little but all the while keeping an eye on the traffic passing through the checkpoint.

The owner kept stepping out, looking forlornly down the street for his delivery of bread. Eventually he made a phone call and Henderson overheard the head baker telling him that the Germans had commandeered the bakery and were sending all bread supplies to their advancing troops.

Minutes later a German from the checkpoint purchased half a dozen coffees and carried them across to his comrades on a tray, returning fifteen minutes later with the empty cups and saucers.

'How's it going, Grenadier?' Henderson asked. 'That sun's a killer.'

The soldier – who, like most German infantrymen, seemed barely out of his teens – smiled. 'You speak good German,' he said.

'I'm an Alsatian,' Henderson lied, by way of explanation. 'I grew up speaking German, though I moved away from the border many years ago.'

'Ahh,' the soldier said uninterestedly.

'We get no news,' Henderson said. 'Do you know what's happening?'

The soldier laughed. 'Do you think I get any more news standing out there than you get sitting in here? All I know is that the tanks are advancing and it's the usual struggle to get enough fuel and food up to our troops to keep things moving.'

Henderson smiled. 'I bet you're happier back here than up at the front.'

'Too bloody right,' the German said, nodding. 'I was one of the first over the border at Sedan. I've had my share of fighting, and hopefully it will be over soon.'

'I hope so too.' Henderson smiled at him.

As the German wandered back to his post the proprietor came across to the table and announced that he was closing.

'You and the Boche are the only custom I've had in the

last two hours,' he explained. 'It's not worth staying open with no bread, no eggs and sausage that's hardly worth the name.'

'Fair enough,' Henderson said, as he grabbed his hat off the table and stood up. 'This bakery – you wouldn't happen to know where it is?'

'Of course,' the proprietor said, as he began lifting chairs on to the tabletops. 'It's less than a kilometre – you must have passed by as you came towards us. But there's no way you'll get any bread. The master baker told me that the Germans are taking every loaf and ordering him to run the ovens flat out. They're threatening to shoot anyone who stops working or asks to go home. He says he'll be out of flour by tomorrow.'

Henderson left a decent tip and Marc followed him outside into the sun as three trucks crammed with troops roared past on the cobbles. They were waved through the checkpoint without slowing down.

'What can we do?' Marc asked, as the pair began walking towards the bakery.

Henderson wanted Marc to start thinking for himself and tested the boy as they walked. 'What did you notice about the checkpoint?'

Marc shrugged. 'They weren't stopping anyone unless they were French.'

'Exactly.' Henderson nodded. 'And any vehicle that

either looked German or had a German at the wheel got waved through. Plus, most of the trucks only had one man in the cab.'

Marc smiled. 'Which makes them easy to pinch if the driver steps out.'

Henderson nodded again. 'The soldier mentioned a basic flaw in the German tactics. It caused them problems in the east last year and with luck it might make our journey across the front line a lot easier than it would have been to cross the trenches during the Great War.'

Marc was confused. 'What flaw?'

'The Germans fight by advancing rapidly with massed armour. Tanks, motorised artillery, etcetera. The trouble with this is that their armour charges ahead, but if it goes too far too fast it outruns the supply lines and ends up stranded without food to feed the men and diesel and ammunition to feed the tanks.'

'Is that why the advance stopped north of Paris for three weeks?' Marc asked.

'That's right. So all we have to do is stop a bread truck or a fuel tanker, bash the driver over the head, put on his tunic and we should be able to get right up the German lines. They're advancing too quickly to build fortifications, so if we find a country lane or a flat field, we might be able to keep right on going into French territory.'

'But won't the French troops shoot when they see us come towards them?'

Henderson nodded. 'Without a doubt,' he said seriously.

CHAPTER THIRTY-ONE

The bakery was one of the most modern in Paris, with a steel-framed building set behind brick walls and three aluminium chimneys venting the smell of warm bread across the neighbourhood. Germans guarded the front gate and an elderly man in a white overall was laid out in the shaded portion of the courtyard, apparently suffering from heat stroke.

At the rear, three trucks stood in line – one German and two requisitioned from local businesses. A procession of soldiers and exhausted-looking bakery workers ran between the rear entrance and the back of the leading truck. Each person carried a basket of hot loaves, which were unceremoniously thrown into the back of the leading truck until it was piled high. All the while an overweight German logistics officer bawled at everyone to work faster.

When the truck was filled, the canvas awning over the back was tied in place to stop the bread toppling out. A German infantryman with his shirt drenched in sweat climbed up to the cab and slammed the door. He wanted to mop the beads of sweat running off his bald head, but as he reached towards the tunic thrown across the passenger seat he noticed the boy crammed into the footwell with a pistol aiming right at him.

'Act normal,' Marc whispered, in his broken German. 'Start the engine and drive or I'll shoot you in the head.'

The perspiring German gave a wary nod as he reached around and slotted a key into the steering column.

'Good man,' Marc said, as the engine growled to life and the cab filled with the pungent aroma of the German's sweat.

Either nervous, incompetent, or both, the German made a hash of lifting the clutch, making the truck shudder as it moved away. This was followed by grinding cogs as he struggled to find second gear.

'I need you to collect a friend,' Marc said, squeezing out of the cramped footwell as they turned left, away from the bakery and out of sight of the other Germans. 'Take the second street on the right and stop by the bridge over the railway line.'

Marc kept the pistol pointing at the German all the while as he pulled himself up on to the passenger seat.

'Turn here,' Marc said, but the German knew and was already slowing down.

Marc looked along the pavement and was pleased to see no signs of life. It was Saturday and the government offices on either side of the street were closed. As the truck rode over the hump of the bridge, Henderson popped out of a hiding place on the embankment that led down to a pair of railway lines. He jogged into the road behind the truck and pulled the driver's door open as it came to a halt.

'Out,' Henderson shouted, waving a German pistol in the soldier's face. 'Don't mess us about. You'll be OK if you stay calm.'

The German stepped from the cab with his hands raised and Henderson told him to walk towards the railing. As soon as he stepped on to the pavement, Henderson put the muzzle of his silenced pistol against the back of the German's head. The shot knocked the soldier forwards and he slumped dead over the railing, exactly as Henderson had hoped.

After pocketing his pistol, Henderson grabbed the German around his thighs and lifted him up. The dead body flopped over the side of the bridge and crashed through a canopy of leaves before landing on the embankment beside the railway with a snap of twigs and the rustle of dead leaves.

'Pass his tunic out,' Henderson said hurriedly, as he rushed back to the truck. 'I'll need that and his helmet to get through the checkpoint.'

*

The fuel gauge showed full and the road leading south towards the German lines was clear. The only traffic they encountered beyond the checkpoint was a column of factory-fresh tanks, heading for their first taste of battle. The bare-chested crews leaned out of the hatches to escape the stifling heat.

Twenty kilometres south of Paris the truck was waved through another checkpoint – with Marc sliding into the footwell – and they finally saw the first proper sign of German presence, in the form of a tented command post with a field hospital behind it. Another couple of kilometres brought them to a line of smouldering farm buildings. Destruction seemed pointless when everyone knew that the Germans were going to win and Marc wondered if the buildings might have caught fire by accident.

Things became more hectic when they reached the edge of German territory. A single-file column of armour almost a kilometre long stood along the road awaiting orders to advance. The tanks were wide and Henderson had to pass slowly, often with a set of wheels running in the grass verge.

The fields beside the tanks were dotted with exhausted French troops. The Germans had captured more than a million French soldiers during the early part of the invasion. But guarding prisoners was a drain on German manpower and feeding them practically impossible. So while French prisoners in the north had spent the past month penned into fields, dying from disease and starvation, soldiers captured now were simply stripped of weapons and equipment and ordered to march south.

The ones who remained were injured or sick and had no option but to suffer in the sun without even water, while their enemy calmly waited to be resupplied before pushing onwards. Marc had seen plenty of suffering during his journey from Beauvais to Paris, but the sight of young soldiers dying of thirst and hunger seemed especially chilling. Beyond this human wreckage, another field was piled high with orderly stacks. Tin helmets, rifles, ammunition, grenades.

Henderson managed a smile. 'When I was a boy, I had a collection of lead soldiers,' he said. 'Before I went to bed, my mother would make me tidy them all up into piles, just like that – only smaller.'

The thoughts of childhood made Marc realise that he

knew nothing about Charles Henderson. 'Do you have a wife or children, sir?'

'I had a daughter, but she died of tuberculosis when she was a baby. My wife took the loss very badly.'

'I'm sorry,' Marc said, shifting uncomfortably in his seat and wishing he hadn't asked.

'She broke down completely at one point,' Henderson admitted. 'We'd like another child, but my spending so much time abroad makes that difficult.'

After passing through a village crowded with German troops, they came to a fork and Henderson picked a dirt road that obviously wasn't the main highway. The lane twisted and trees overhung from either side, creating a dappled shade.

'I think we're past the last of the Germans,' Henderson said, driving as quickly as he dared.

Marc dived off his seat when they came to a clearing from which an artillery piece aimed straight at them. Henderson realised that they were French.

'Marc, get up and hold the wheel,' he shouted frantically, remembering that he was still wearing a German tunic and pulling it down his arms.

As Marc steered, the French soldiers began to shout and Henderson slowed down. It was fortunate that they'd taken one of the commandeered French trucks, because a German army vehicle would have caused outright hostility rather than suspicion.

'Lean out of the window so they can see you're a child,' Henderson ordered.

Marc did as he was told and shouted, 'We're not Boche! We're not Boche!' over and over.

Three French soldiers came out of hedges alongside, their rifles pointing at Marc and Henderson. Henderson slowed the truck to a halt, but kept the engine running and a foot on the accelerator in case things got rough.

'What's in the back?' a bearded French sergeant demanded, as he pushed the butt of his rifle through the window beside Marc's head.

'Fresh bread sir,' Marc said.

At the rear, another soldier had ripped open the canvas awning and found himself under bombardment from hundreds of loaves, bouncing into the dirt before rolling off down the hill.

'Where is this bread from?' the sergeant aiming the gun demanded.

'They commandeered my truck and forced us to drive from Paris,' Henderson lied. 'We killed the German who was sent with us and decided to try finding our way through the lines.'

There seemed to be six troops in total and they were running into the road and tearing hungrily into the fresh loaves. This irritated the sergeant who was questioning Henderson.

'Where's your discipline?' the sergeant shouted at the soldiers. 'Get back under cover.'

'There's more than a hundred German tanks just a couple of kilometres from here,' Henderson said. 'They're gearing up ready for another push. If we clear some of the bread out of the back, you could all ride with us.'

'No thanks,' the sergeant sneered. 'The rest of our regiment surrendered this morning. Us six decided to stand and fight. But we'll take some bread if that's OK.'

Henderson was almost too stunned to speak as the sergeant stepped off the running board of the truck and lowered his rifle. 'Panzer tanks have got twice the range of that artillery piece,' he explained. 'They'll take one look through their binoculars and blast you out of the road.'

The sergeant looked down at his boots like a little boy in a lot of trouble. 'Germans bombed my house,' he explained. 'Wife, mother and two daughters, all dead. Most of us have some experience like that. I'd sooner get blasted than look any Boche in the eye and call him sir.'

'Are you sure all your men feel the same way?' Henderson asked.

The sergeant stepped back from the truck and

shouted, 'The nice fellow here says there's two hundred tanks coming our way and he's offering you a ride south. If any of you want to take it, go right ahead.'

The hungry soldiers had mouths stuffed with bread, but they all shook their heads.

Marc didn't know whether to be impressed by their bravery or appalled at their stupidity.

'Well, good luck then – I guess,' Henderson said. 'If you've taken all the bread you need I'll get going. Do you know if there are any more Germans south of here?'

The sergeant shook his head. 'I reckon all you'll find is empty French positions and soldiers with tails between their legs.'

As Henderson drove away he heard someone banging on the side of the truck and pulled up. He expected someone to say they'd changed heart and wanted to climb in the back, but instead a skinny lad stepped on to the running board beside Marc and jabbed a sheet of paper through the window.

'I don't have an envelope or a stamp, but the address is at the top of the paper and I reckon you've got a better chance of getting it to my wife than I have.'

Marc was startled. The soldier seemed more like one of the older lads from the orphanage than someone with a wife.

'I'll do what I can,' Marc said.

Henderson shook his head as they drove on beneath the hanging branches. 'War does funny things to people,' he sighed. 'Mad bastards.'

CHAPTER THIRTY-TWO

The diesel-powered truck had seen better days and the engine became unhappy at anything over fifty kilometres per hour. Henderson had resigned himself to fate and didn't bother to hurry: if Herr Potente had arrived before his message and taken the children, there was nothing he could do.

Every so often, Marc would climb through to the back of the truck and pass loaves to the hungry soldiers lining the road, but Henderson told him to close the canopy whenever they got into traffic because he didn't want to risk getting mobbed. They stopped and ate a good meal in Blois, courtesy of a restaurant run by an Englishman who was an old friend of Henderson.

The restaurateur knew a local farmer who had a supply

of diesel and Henderson paid two gold ingots for a twenty-litre drum. It was an exorbitant price, but with fuel so scarce he was pleased to have found any at all and now he had enough to drive all the way to Bordeaux.

The sky was turning dark as they crossed the bridge into Tours. Henderson stopped at the first church he came to, but they had to wait a quarter-hour for the evening mass to finish before they could ask the priest for the location of his retired colleague who'd taken in a pair of orphans.

The priest drew directions on a scrap of notepaper and although they were slightly ambiguous, the truck reached the little farmhouse within half an hour. Henderson drove on past the house and switched off the headlamps and the engine as he rolled up to a metal gate. He took out the silenced pistol and spoke to Marc as he replaced the bullet he'd fired earlier in the day.

'If the Germans intercepted our message they could be waiting for me. So I'll approach from the side and cut across the field to the rear of the house.'

'Shall I cover your back?' Marc asked.

Henderson shook his head. 'I've been trained to move quietly. Stay here, and if you hear shooting, or if I'm not back within an hour, you'd better clear out.'

Marc didn't like the sound of this. If something happened to Henderson he'd be back on his own in the middle of nowhere. Although at least he'd have thirteen gold ingots and a gun.

Henderson jumped out of the van and dug his fingers into the earth. He daubed mud on to his cheeks and forehead before disappearing into a potato patch, crouching low as he surveyed the outside of the house. There were no suspicious cars and only one light on inside, so he crept towards the back door.

As Henderson stepped clear of the potatoes, he heard a sob. He turned and saw the outline of a boy. He was slender and he sat with a sketchpad on his lap, although it was too dark to draw.

'Paul Clarke?' Henderson whispered.

The boy's head turned around and his teeth caught the moonlight as his mouth dropped open. 'Henderson, is that you?'

Another sob sent a chill down Henderson's back. 'Are the Germans here or something?' Henderson asked. 'Tell me, what's the matter?'

*

Half an hour later Marc and Henderson were inside the house, sitting around the dining table drinking mugs of hot milk. Yvette had scrubbed the blood from where Hugo died, but Rosie had picked a bundle of wild flowers and laid them against the dresser.

'We'll head south to Bordeaux,' Henderson said. 'I've

heard there are still regular sailings for the Cornish coast
– although that was a few days back, so we'll have to see.'

Marc was half listening and half watching Rosie. Girls
fascinated him and she looked sad, with her long hair
mussed and the soles of her feet dirty where she'd been
outside feeding the chickens.

'What did you do with Herr Potente's body?'
Henderson asked the adults.

'We spoke to the police. They made a report and took
both bodies away,' Yvette explained.

'Dammit,' Henderson said. Then he seemed to change
the subject. 'Have you lived on this farm for long?'

'It's a family farm,' Father Doran explained. 'It
belonged to our parents and our grandparents
before them.'

'You'll have to leave before the Germans get here,'
Henderson said. 'The Gestapo know where Herr Potente
was sent and they'll most likely uncover the police report.
They'll interrogate you about the plans and about my
whereabouts.'

'But we know very little, and by then, hopefully, you'll
be long gone,' Yvette said.

'I know that,' Henderson said. 'But the Gestapo will
want to be sure and they'll make sure by torturing you.'

Marc bared his teeth. 'Look what those animals did to
my tooth,' he said. 'I heard the Oberst's orders: Potente

was to interrogate Paul and Rosie and then kill them.'

'I'll not leave my home,' Father Doran said resolutely, as he noisily set his mug on the table. 'I'm too old to hide under staircases. The sooner I die in this world, the sooner I'll join with God.'

Henderson looked frustrated. 'I'm sure your faith is a comfort, Father, but what about your sister?'

Yvette shook her head. 'Mr Henderson, why don't you worry about the plans and getting the children home safely? My brother and I can worry for ourselves.'

*

Henderson shared the double bed with Paul, while Marc made the best of Hugo's cushions and Rosie bunked in with Yvette. Marc came downstairs at what seemed an early hour, only to find that Yvette had been up for long enough to pluck and roast a chicken for their journey south and prepare a decent spread for breakfast.

Father Doran had already been out to milk his two cows; Henderson was studying a road map; whilst Paul and Rosie sat at the table, picking at food and looking sad.

'Hello, Marc.' Rosie smiled at him. 'How did you sleep?'

'Not so bad,' he answered. 'But Henderson snores like hell.'

'Tell me about it,' Paul moaned. 'I was in the same bed as him and my pillow was vibrating.'

Henderson looked up and smiled slightly, but went back to his map without speaking.

'Do you need any help, Yvette?' Rosie asked, as the old lady packed sliced bread and a pot of homemade jam into a wicker basket.

'I'm almost done,' Yvette said. 'There's plenty of food for the journey. I've left the chicken on top because it's still warm and underneath there's bread, cheese, yogurt, some of my paté and bottles of fresh milk.'

'There's enough there to feed an army,' Henderson said, smiling. 'You're really too kind.'

'The way these two eat it won't last long, and I'd bet young Marc is just the same.'

'Eats like a horse,' Henderson agreed. Then he glanced at his watch. 'I reckon we'll be leaving in a few minutes. So now's the time to say your goodbyes, go to the loo and make sure you've packed everything.'

The Clarkes both went and got their cases from upstairs. Rosie went straight out to throw hers in the back of the truck, but Paul approached Yvette and handed her a drawing. It showed himself, Rosie and Hugo standing in front of the cottage. Yvette stood at the window inside and Father Doran was depicted running after an escaped chicken.

'Oh,' Yvette gasped, 'it's beautiful.'

Marc caught a quick glance of it before immediately

standing up to see the drawing properly. 'That's awesome,' he said. 'You're like a proper artist or something.'

Paul was modest and tried not to smile too much. 'I did it yesterday, after Hugo . . .'

Yvette put her hand on the back of Paul's neck and kissed him on the forehead. 'I just know you'll be a great artist some day,' she said proudly. 'I'm going to miss you – your sister too.'

Yvette started to sob just as Rosie came in and within a couple of minutes they were all at it. Even Father Doran put down his newspaper and gave Paul and Rosie a tearful hug before wishing Henderson good luck.

'Father, you think about what I said,' Henderson warned, as he stood in the doorway holding the case containing Mannstein's documents. 'You're respected in these parts and I'm sure many people will help you to hide.'

'Perhaps,' Father Doran said calmly. 'Who knows where this war will leave any of us?'

CHAPTER THIRTY-THREE

Henderson rode up front with all three kids in the back, sitting on the luggage with old blankets and cushions donated by Yvette for comfort. He'd grown to like Marc and missed having him in the passenger seat alongside him, but he could overhear fragments of the three youngsters' conversation and was pleased to hear Marc acting like an ordinary boy as Paul tried to show him how to draw a tank.

It was three hundred and thirty kilometres to Bordeaux. A decent car would have made it in six and a half hours, but the van took ten. The kids left the canvas tarp at the back open so that they could see, but they hardly bothered to look out. They'd all spent days on the road and there were only so many times you could be shocked by a soldier on crutches or a grandma lying dead in a ditch. For Marc – who hadn't ventured beyond the orphanage and its surrounding farms until ten days earlier – carnage almost seemed like the natural state of things.

*

They reached Bordeaux as it was starting to turn dark. Henderson's fingers were numb from being wrapped around the steering wheel all day and his calves ached from working the foot pedals, but his heart was warmed by the sight of a small passenger ship in the harbour, flying the British ensign.

Marc felt a touch lost as he stepped out of the truck and saw palm trees growing in front of a hotel. It was warmer here than in northern France and the low buildings with balconies were very different to the offices and apartment blocks of Paris.

'Grab all your kit,' Henderson said hurriedly, pointing at the small stack of bags and cases inside the truck. 'The funnels are smoking, so I'd say that ship is stoking up to leave.'

'How long?' Marc asked, as he passed the bags out of the truck to Rosie.

'An hour if we're lucky. We still have to clear customs and buy tickets – what's more, it could easily be fully booked and Marc doesn't have a passport.'

With two bags each, the foursome crossed a busy road and caught the smell of the sea as they made their way towards the passenger terminal. The building was long and low, with floor to ceiling windows, counters for buying tickets and a roped-off area that led to a customs post where French officials inspected documents and stamped passports. From there, passengers passed on to the dockside and up the gangplanks to board the ship.

As Henderson led the three children inside the building, he looked out and saw a net filled with baggage being hoisted up by a deck crane and one of the two gangplanks being drawn aboard the ship.

'Tickets and passports at the ready, sir,' a steward said in English. His hat bore the name SS *Cardiff Bay* and his Mancunian accent made Henderson feel a little closer to home, but his stomach churned, because the ship was about to leave.

'We've just got here,' Henderson gasped, as he retrieved his passport and wallet from a briefcase. 'I need four tickets.'

At the same time, Rosie had found Paul's passport and her own.

'John,' the steward shouted, 'what's the passenger count?'

'There's a few cabins and plenty of seats.'

Henderson smiled. 'I was worried that you might be full.'

The steward shook his head. 'If you'd been here a week back you'd have seen a right scrum. But the Government laid on some extra boats and we're just picking up stragglers now. I tell you what, since we're about to leave, I'll let you pay the steward on board. Be sure that you do, mind.'

Henderson nodded. 'Of course. Thank you, sir.'

The steward waved them on to the next counter, where a more senior crewmember stood waiting to inspect the passports.

'I only see three,' he said, raising an eyebrow and glancing at Marc.

'His father was killed in an air raid, the documents were all destroyed.'

'I'm sorry, sir, but we have strict regulations to prevent German agents from entering Britain. Every passenger *must* have proper documentation.'

'But he's just a child,' Henderson spluttered.

'I know what you're saying sir, but rules are rules. Especially in wartime. You'll have to apply for a passport from the consular office in town. It opens at nine tomorrow.'

Marc didn't understand English and had to ask Rosie to explain what was going on.

'When will the next boat be here?' Henderson asked.

'We're the only boat running this route now,' the officer said. 'If things go to schedule, we'll be back here Tuesday morning and set to sail Tuesday afternoon.'

Henderson tried to think fast. He knew there was no point trying to throw his weight around, because as a spy he carried no documentation that proved his rank. He felt a tug on his sleeve and saw Marc look up at him.

'Don't worry about me,' Marc said. 'I'll survive on my own.'

Henderson shook his head resolutely. 'Don't be bloody daft, boy,' he said. 'I wouldn't dream of leaving you.'

A great klaxon blasted out on the dockside and a shout of *All aboard* went up. Henderson was in a full-on panic.

'Paul, Rosie,' he said, 'this is your chance. Take your things and the documents and get on board. When you arrive in Britain, ask to speak to Miss Eileen McAfferty at the Home Office, sixty-four Kensington High Street. Tell her what's happened and I promise she'll look after you.'

There was a mix-up over whose stuff was in each bag as Henderson made sure that Rosie had enough French francs to buy her tickets and two pound notes for when she arrived in Britain. She quickly kissed Henderson on the forehead and raced towards the French officials, who stood up and waved the two children through.

'Run, run,' they urged.

The crew was ready to pull in the last gangplank as the Clarkes chased across the dockside. They made the ramp with a heavy bag in each arm and the last of the ship's crew behind them.

Back in the terminal Henderson turned to Marc and smiled. 'Hopefully we can find a room for the night, then we'll go and see the consul in the morning.'

'OK.' Marc said, nodding. 'I owe you.'

Henderson realised his companion was a touch blurry-eyed and he put an arm around the boy's back.

'Did you really think I'd abandon you after everything we've been through?'

EPILOGUE

Paul hated the sea. He'd crossed the English Channel many times, always with a green face poised over a sick bag and his father telling him that it was better out than in. The prospect of a far longer voyage from Bordeaux to Plymouth filled him with dread.

The ship was dilapidated and the corridors were blacked out to avoid detection by Germans at night. This meant the cabin stewards had to show passengers to their cabins by torchlight. As they walked, the prop shaft ran at full speed, making noise and vibration that was close to unbearable.

'You've got a blackout curtain over your porthole,' the steward said. 'Once it gets dark, don't open it – don't even touch it. The tiniest chink of light is all the Boche need to spot us in the night. There's U-boats[6] on the prowl, so we'll be going flat out whenever the sea lets us, but that makes for a choppy ride. I recommend you stay in your cabin as much as you can. There's a canteen up on the next deck, but there's no food till morning. I'll be down with tea and hot water in about an hour.'

The metal door of the tiny cabin squealed and Paul was knocked back by the smell of cigarettes. The beds were filthy, the bin overflowing and the sliding door leading to a toilet and washbasin hung off its runners.

'Sorry about the state of the cabin, but we've been running back and forth for two weeks without time for the cleaners to come aboard.'

'Don't worry,' Rosie said, smiling bravely as the steward flicked a switch to turn on a tiny light bulb. 'It's a ride home and that's all that matters.'

Paul sat on the lower bunk as the door clanged shut and thought about England. While Rosie called it home, he could only remember living in Paris. The swaying was already making him feel sick and he knew it would get worse once they reached open sea.

'I might go up on deck and get some air,' he said.

Rosie shook her head. 'You heard the steward. You can't go walking up on deck when there's no light.'

'Twenty-three hours, turning my guts out,' Paul moaned.

---

[6] U-boat – a German submarine.

Then he looked thoughtful. 'That Marc kid seemed pretty nice. I hope Henderson gets him a passport.'

'I'm sure he will,' Rosie said. 'He's well connected.'

'And the way you two were chattering in the back of the truck,' Paul teased. 'You're such a flirt.'

'Give over,' Rosie tutted. 'I was just being nice to him.'

'If I hadn't been there you'd have been kissing or something.'

Rosie wagged her finger in her brother's face. 'Don't think you can wind me up just because you're queasy,' she said. 'I'll still smack you one.'

Suddenly there was a booming sound and the ship rose up as if it had been picked out of the water. Then, just as sharply, the invisible hand let go.

'What was that?' Paul gulped, as all the lights flickered.

A second bang tilted the boat forwards and this time there was an ear-splitting explosion, magnified by the metal walls and decks all around. The lights went out for good and a siren sounded in the corridor as a crackly announcement broke over the tannoy:

'All passengers collect your life jackets and move on to the deck. I repeat, all passengers collect your life jackets and move on to the deck.'

'Where are they?' Rosie shouted anxiously.

Paul remembered the Titanic and how there hadn't been enough safety equipment, but Rosie found the life jackets under the bed and quickly pulled the stiff yellow bib over her head.

Outside, the steward was banging on the cabin doors shouting, 'All out, all out. Everyone on deck!'

Rosie grabbed the case containing the documents and stepped into the hallway, which was suddenly crammed with passengers queuing to climb the narrow staircase up to the main deck.

'What's happened?' Rosie asked desperately.

'Air raid,' someone shouted. 'Didn't you hear the planes?'

But they'd heard nothing over the grinding of the prop shaft.

'Leave your bags,' the steward ordered as he grabbed the case containing the documents from Rosie's hand and threw them back inside the cabin.

'They're important,' Rosie said, as the queue moved forwards towards the steps.

'Don't be stupid, girl,' the steward said unsympathetically, as he barged on through the passengers. 'People are important.'

Life seemed increasingly cheap but Rosie knew he was right, as she looked back to make sure that Paul was still behind her.

The dive bomber had hit the Cardiff Bay less than five kilometres out of Bordeaux, in the broad channel that led from the port to the Atlantic Ocean. The ancient steamer was steadily tilting forwards as water poured through a hole in the bow.

As Rosie made it up the near-vertical steps and into the twilight, she looked along the deck and saw that the bow was already touching the waterline and the stern was way out of the water. The passengers stood on deck in their life jackets as the crew pulled tarps away from the lifeboats and began the clumsy process of lowering them over the side into a mercifully calm sea.

Below decks, the seawater reached the boiler room in the heart of the ship. As it rushed into the furnaces, the mass of water hit flaming coals and the result was superheated steam. Horrific screams echoed from below as men boiled alive and the extraordinary pressure ruptured one of the funnels and blew several deck hatches into the air.

Rosie grabbed Paul tight as the air filled with the tang of burning paint and hot metal. High above, a German Stuka had started a near vertical bombing run. Its bombs missed by more than twenty metres, but a series of underwater explosions threw the ship to one side. The hull levelled off, but this was a false dawn and a mass of water rebounded towards the front of the ship and dragged the bow underwater.

There was a deathly grinding noise as the front of the ship sank. Screams came from all around as people charged towards the stern, grabbing whatever they could hold on to as the angle of the deck grew steeper.

Many seemed to hope for a miracle, but Rosie was a realist and she knew they were going down.

'We either jump now or go down with it,' she shouted, grabbing her brother by his life jacket and straddling the handrail as adults charged past in one direction, whilst an increasing amount of debris barrelled down the deck towards them.

The hull had been more than fifteen metres out of the water when Paul and Rosie boarded, but the old steamer was plunging like a torpedo and they touched water the instant they were over the handrail.

Rosie was an excellent swimmer, but Paul's stroke was weak and she held on to his life jacket and begged him to kick. The jackets made them buoyant, but the rapidly sinking ship created a vortex under the water that was dragging them down.

After half a minute of fighting to get away and as more desperate souls threw themselves into the water, the stern of the Cardiff Bay went under, leaving a great circular depression into which everyone and everything was sucked. The epicentre was less than ten metres from the Clarkes and the twisting water flipped one of the few lifeboats to have been successfully launched. A dozen passengers were trapped under the upturned hull as it was sucked down.

As a huge air bubble blew out of the depression, a powerful current gripped Rosie's legs and pulled her deep underwater. She tried keeping hold of Paul, but it was pitch black and they broke apart when a wooden oar smashed her in the back. She reached in all directions, but he was gone.

The urge to breathe was becoming overpowering and Rosie was sure that she'd drown. While the cold water made her skin feel as if it was filled with needles, she knew she'd die if she didn't surface quickly.

Then, as swiftly as the current had swept her under, the

water around Rosie became still. No bubbles, no chunks of debris, and she felt the life jacket start to pull under her arms. The current rushed against her body as she came back to the surface and she put her ankles together and arms at her side to streamline her shape.

Her ears popped as she broke the surface and took the biggest breath of her life. But her relief was short-lived.

'Paul,' she screamed, as she gulped air and spun around, studying the debris and bobbing heads on the flat plane of water surrounding her. The nearest was a fit-looking fifteen year old with curls of black hair stuck to his face. He ploughed through the water towards Rosie and took it upon himself to rescue her.

'Are you hurt?' he asked, in French tinged by a slight American accent.

But Rosie was frantic for her brother. 'Paul!' she screamed. 'Paul, where the hell are you?'

'Calm down, save your breath,' the American said firmly. 'Did Paul have his life jacket on?'

'Of course!' Rosie said.

'We all got sucked down. He could have surfaced a hundred metres from here. How about you? Are you OK?'

Rosie nodded as she kicked her legs gently under the water. 'Something hit me in the back, but it's not that bad.'

'Name's PT,' the teenager said. 'Hold on to me and we'll be just fine. We're probably less than a kilometre from the coast.'

Rosie glanced around and while she could hear distant cries, there seemed to be no one else nearby. Her eyes were close to the water and all she could see was the moon and a few buildings lit up along the coastline.

'I guess the current pulled us some distance,' Rosie said.

'I'm a good swimmer and you don't look bad yourself,' PT said. 'We can make it to shore, but the cold will do us in if we hang about.'

A tear welled in Rosie's eye as the life-jacketed pair started swimming towards the coast. Images flashed through her mind like fireworks: Mannstein's documents lying on the riverbed, her mother white and thin the day before she died of cancer, her father coughing blood, Hugo's last gasp and Yvette's smile as Paul handed her his beautiful drawing before leaving the cottage that morning.

She looked across at the young American.

'I hope my brother's out there somewhere,' Rosie choked. 'He's all I have left.'

Read on for the exclusive first chapter of the next book in the Henderson's Boys series, *Eagle Day* . . .

CHAPTER ONE

It was eleven at night, but the port of Bordeaux crackled with life. Refugee kids slumped in humid alleyways, using their mothers' bellies for pillows. Drunken soldiers and marooned sailors scrapped, sang and peed against blacked-out streetlamps. Steamers lined up three abreast at the wharves, waiting for a coal train that showed no sign of arriving soon.

With roads clogged and no diesel for trucks, the dockside was choked with produce while people went hungry less than twenty kilometres away. Meat and veg surrendered to maggots, while recently arrived boats had nowhere to unload and ditched rotting cargo into the sea.

A man and a boy strode along the dock wall, alongside rusting bollards and oranges catching moonlight as they bobbed in the water between a pair of Indian cargo ships.

'Will the consulate be open this late?' Marc Kilgour asked.

Marc was twelve. He was well built, with a scruffy blond tangle down his brow and his shirt clutched over his nose to mask the sickly odour of rotting bananas. The pigskin bag over Marc's shoulder held everything he owned.

Charles Henderson walked beside him: six feet of wiry muscle and a face that would look better after a night's sleep and an encounter with a sharp blade. Disguised as peasants, the pair wore corduroy trousers and white shirts damp with sweat. A suitcase strained Henderson's right arm and the metal objects inside jangled as he grabbed Marc's collar and yanked him off course.

'Look where you're putting your feet!'

Marc looked back and saw that his oversized boot had been saved from a mound of human shit. With a hundred thousand refugees in town it was a common enough sight, but Marc's stomach still recoiled. A second later he kicked the outstretched leg of a young woman with dead eyes and bandaged toes.

'Pardon me,' Marc said, but she didn't even notice. The woman had drunk herself into a stupor and no one would bat an eye if she turned up dead at sunrise.

Since running away from his orphanage two weeks earlier, Marc had trained himself to block out the horrible things he saw all around: from mumbling old dears suffering heat stroke to escaped pigs lapping the blood around corpses at the roadside.

The port was under blackout, so Henderson didn't see Marc's sad eyes, but he sensed a shudder in the boy's breathing and pressed a hand against his back.

'What can we do, mate?' Henderson asked soothingly. 'There's millions of them . . . You have to look after number one.'

Marc found comfort in Henderson's hand, which made him think of the parents he'd never known.

'If I get to England, what happens?' Marc asked nervously. He wanted to add, *Can I live with you?* but choked on the words.

They turned away from the dockside, on to a street lined with warehouses. Clumps of refugees from the north sat under corrugated canopies designed to keep goods dry as they were loaded on to trucks. Despite the late hour a half-dozen boys played a rowdy game of football, using cabbages stolen from the wharves.

Henderson ignored Marc's tricky question, instead answering the one he'd asked two minutes earlier.

'The consulate will be closed, but we have nowhere to stay and the office is sure to be inundated by morning. We might be able to find our own way in . . .'

Henderson tailed off as a pair of German planes swept overhead. The lads playing cabbage football made machine-gun noises and hurled curses over the sea, until their parents yelled at them to cut the racket before it woke younger siblings.

'I'm French,' Marc noted seriously. 'I don't speak a word of English, so how can you get me a British passport?'

'We'll manage,' Henderson said confidently, as he stopped walking for a moment and switched his heavy case from one arm to the other. 'After all we've been through, you should trust me by now.'

The consulate was only a kilometre from the dockside, but Henderson insisted he knew better than the directions jotted down by an official at the passenger terminal. They traipsed muggy streets where the smell of sewage mixed with sea air, until a friendly-but-sozzled dockworker set them back on the right path.

'I wonder where Paul and Rosie are,' Marc said, as they broke into a cobbled square with a crumbling fountain at its centre.

'They'll be upriver, close to open sea by now,' Henderson reckoned, after a glance at his watch. 'There's U-boats[1] prowling and the captain will want to reach the English Channel before daylight.'

A courthouse spanned one side of the square, with a domed church opposite and a couple of gendarmes[2]

---

[1] U-boat – a German submarine.
[2] Gendarmes – French police officers.

standing watch, their main purpose apparently to stop refugees settling on the church steps. The British consulate stood in a neat terrace of offices, jewellers, pawnbrokers and banks.

One end of this row had suffered structural damage from a bomb meant for the docks. Even in moonlight you could see the dramatically warped façade above a jeweller's shop and broken roof slates swept to a tidy pile at the side.

With low-flying bombers and the German forces expected to reach Bordeaux within the week, the Union Jack flag had tactfully been removed from the consulate, but nothing could be done about the British lions woven into wrought-iron gates padlocked across the front door.

Several of His Majesty's subjects gathered on the front steps, with noticeably better clothing and luggage than the refugees scavenging food along the dockside, but Henderson was wary. The Gestapo[3] were still after him and they could easily have spies watching what remained of Bordeaux's British community.

Henderson would stand out amongst the other Brits in his peasant clothing and Marc spoke no English, so rather than join the queue and wait for nine a.m., he led Marc around the rear of the terrace and was pleased to find that it backed on to a sheltered alleyway. The

---

[3]Gestapo – German secret police.

bombing had fractured a water pipe beneath the cobbles and their boots swilled through several centimetres of water.

'Have you still got my torch?' Henderson whispered, when they reached the rear door of the consulate.

The batteries were weak and the beam faltered as Marc scanned the brickwork. After snatching his torch Henderson squatted down and aimed light through the letterbox.

'Nobody home,' he said, as the metal flap snapped shut. 'No sign of an alarm, no bars at the windows. If I give you a boost, do you reckon you can get yourself through the small window?'

Marc craned his head up as Henderson aimed the torch so that he could see.

'What about the two cops in the square?' Marc asked. 'They'll hear if the glass goes.'

Henderson shook his head. 'It's a sash window; you should be able to force it open with a lever.'

Henderson stepped back out of the puddle and found dry cobbles on which to lay and open his case. Marc noticed shadowy figures passing the end of the alleyway, then jolted at the distinctive click of Henderson loading his pistol.

Marc was delighted that a British agent was going to all this bother on his account. Henderson could have abandoned him at the passenger terminal and sailed aboard the *Cardiff Bay* with Paul and Rosie. But as well as a soft heart, Henderson had a ruthless streak and the gun made Marc uneasy.

In the three days since Marc first met Henderson in Paris, Henderson had shot or blown up half a dozen Germans and machine-gunned a grovelling Frenchman in his bathtub. If the next figure at the end of the alleyway chose to come and investigate, Marc knew Henderson would kill them without a thought.

Henderson passed over a crowbar before screwing a silencer to the front of his pistol. Marc ran his hand along the oiled bar and glimpsed inside the suitcase: ammunition, a compact machine gun, a zipped pouch in which Marc knew lay gold ingots and a stack of French currency. The clothes and toilet bag seemed like an afterthought, squeezed into the bottom right corner. Marc found it miraculous that Henderson could lift all this, let alone carry it several kilometres through the port.

After fastening leather buckles and tipping the jangling case back on its side, Henderson faced the building and lowered his knee into the puddle. Marc leaned against the wall and stepped up so that his wet boots balanced on Henderson's shoulders.

'Now I'm really glad you didn't tread in that pile of turds,' Henderson noted.

Despite nerves and his precarious position astride

Henderson's shoulders, Marc snorted with laughter.

'Don't make me giggle,' he said firmly, walking his hands up the brickwork as Henderson stood, raising Marc level with the landing window between ground and first floors.

Marc rested his chest against the wall, then took the crowbar from his back pocket.

'You're heavier than you look,' Henderson huffed, as Marc's unsteady boots tore at his skin.

The oak window frame was rotting and Henderson felt a shower of flaking paint as Marc dug the forked tongue of the crowbar under the frame and pushed as hard as he dared. The catch locking the two sliding panes together was strong, but the two screws holding it in place lifted easily from the dried-out wood.

'Gotcha,' Marc whispered triumphantly, as he threw the window open.

To Henderson's relief, Marc's weight shifted as the boy pulled himself through the window. He crashed down on to plush carpet inside, narrowly avoiding a vase and a knock-out encounter with the banister.

Beeswax and old varnish filled Marc's nose as he hurried downstairs. The building was small, but its pretensions were grand and paintings of wigged men and naval battles lined the short flight of steps down to the back door.

Henderson grabbed his suitcase as Marc pulled across

two heavy bolts and opened the back door. Beyond the stairwell the ground floor comprised a single large room. They moved amongst desks and cabinets, separated from the waiting area at the opposite end by an ebony countertop and spiralled gold rails.

Marc was fascinated by the tools of bureaucracy: typewriters, rubber stamps, carbon papers and hole punches.

'So they keep blank passports here?' Marc asked, as he stared at the banks of wooden drawers along one wall.

'If they haven't run out,' Henderson said, as he slammed his heavy case on a desktop, tilting a stack of envelopes on to the parquet floor. 'But we can't make a passport without a photograph.'

Henderson pulled a leather wallet out of his case. The miniature photographic kit comprised a matchbox-sized pinhole camera, tiny vials of photographic chemicals and sheets of photographic paper large enough to produce the kind of pictures used in identity documents.

'Go stand under the wall clock,' Henderson said, as he worked with the tiny camera, inserting a small rectangle of photographic paper.

Henderson looked up and saw a peculiar mix of apprehension and emotion on Marc's face.

'Nobody ever took my photograph before,' he admitted.

Henderson looked surprised. 'Not at the school or the orphanage?'

Marc shook his head.

'We've got very little light,' Henderson explained, as he propped the camera on a stack of ledgers. 'So I need you to stay *absolutely* still and keep your eyes open.'

Marc stood rigid for twenty seconds, then rushed forwards on Henderson's signal.

'When can I see it?' he asked, as he blinked his stinging eyes repeatedly.

'I have a developing kit,' Henderson explained. 'There must be a kitchen somewhere. I need you to find me three saucers and some warm water.'

As Marc raced upstairs to find the kitchen, Henderson began looking around the offices for blank passports. He discovered an entire drawer full of them, along with a wooden cigar box containing all the necessary stamps and, most helpfully, a crumpled blue manual detailing the correct procedure for dealing with a consular passport application.

One of the telephones rang, but Henderson ignored it and began shaking his photographic chemicals, ready for when Marc came back with the water.

A second phone thrummed as Marc came downstairs with three saucers and a tobacco tin filled with hot tap water. Henderson found the ringing irritating, but with France in chaos it didn't surprise him that the consular phones would ring through the night.

'I need absolute darkness to develop the photograph,'

Henderson explained, as he spread out the three saucers and dipped a fragile glass thermometer in the hot water. 'Get the lights.'

Once the office lights were out and the blinds at the rear adjusted to shield the moonlight, Henderson gathered his saucers of chemicals in tight formation, leaned forwards over the desk and flipped the jacket he'd been carrying in his suitcase over his head, protecting his equipment from any remaining light.

Marc watched as Henderson fidgeted mysteriously beneath the jacket and the sweet smell of developing fluid filled the air. He stripped the rectangle of photographic paper from the camera and counted the ticks of his watch to ensure it spent the correct time in the developing fluid.

Marc had no idea how long it would be before Henderson emerged with the developed photograph. He thought of asking, but didn't want to affect Henderson's concentration.

'Have you ever made a cup of tea, Marc?' Henderson asked, once he'd moved the sliver of paper from the developer into the bleaching solution.

'Sorry . . .' Marc said weakly. 'I've never even drunk it.'

'You're a blank canvas, Marc Kilgour,' Henderson laughed. 'You go upstairs, put a kettle on the stove and I'll show you how to make a proper English cuppa while your picture dries.'

'What's a cuppa?' Marc asked, liking the word, even if he wasn't sure what it meant.

Henderson trembled with laughter beneath the jacket.

He didn't laugh for long, though. Both phones had stopped ringing, but it became clear from a loud scuffling sound that something was happening on the steps out front.

'Those gendarmes must have heard us breaking in,' Marc said anxiously, as the metal gates over the front door whined for a shot of oil. 'I bet it was them on the phone.'

Henderson remained calm. 'Ignore your emotions and use your brain,' he said firmly as he pulled his head out from beneath the jacket. 'The police don't phone up and ask burglars if they'd be kind enough to leave and the Germans certainly wouldn't tip us off with a fracas on the doorstep. I just need half a minute now to fix the image. Go up to the front window and tell me what you see.'

Marc vaulted the counter and dodged two lines of chairs in the waiting room, then peeked through a tiny crack in the velvet curtains. A white Jaguar sports car had parked up on the cobbles and an anxious crowd hassled its female driver as she unlocked the gates.

'Guessing it's someone who works here,' Marc hissed. 'She's got keys and everyone in the queue's giving her stress.'

Marc could hear what was being said, but it was all in English so he didn't have a clue.

'I have urgent consular business,' the woman yelled. 'You all need to come back in the morning. We're open normal office hours. Nine to five and noon on Saturday.'

Marc ducked behind chairs as the woman squeezed through the front door and told the people outside to mind their fingers before banging it shut.

As soon as she flicked on the lights she saw Henderson. He'd finished developing Marc's photograph and stood behind the counter with his arms out wide to make it clear that he was no threat.

'I'm sorry to startle you like this, Madame. The name's Henderson. Charles Henderson.'

Marc studied the woman from his position crouching behind the chairs. She was in her twenties, and nearly six feet tall. She wore the white blouse and pleated skirt of an office girl, but sculpted black hair and an elegant gold watch gave the impression that she lived off somewhat more than an office girl's salary.

'Charles Henderson,' the woman said knowingly. 'I decoded a transcript from London. Quite a few people are looking for you. Of course, if you're *really* Henderson, you'll know his code word.'

'Seraphim,' Henderson answered, as the woman placed her bag on the countertop then kicked on a wooden panel and ducked under. Marc's eyebrows shot up as he sighted the tops of her stockings.

'I do beg your pardon, but young Marc here needs a passport. We did a bit of damage to your landing window but it's easily fixed . . .'

'Forgive me,' the woman said, making a quick glance back at Marc before cutting Henderson dead with a raised hand. 'My name is Maxine Clere, clerical assistant to the consul. Please make use of our facilities . . . It looks like you've found the blank passports already. I know your work is important, but I have to make immediate contact with London on the scrambled telephone. We've lost the *Cardiff Bay* on the River Garonne, less than thirty kilometres out of Bordeaux – and many are dead.'

CHERUB: Brigands M.C.

Every CHERUB agent comes from somewhere. Dante Scott still has nightmares about the death of his family, brutally killed by a biker gang.

When Dante joins James and Lauren Adams on a mission to infiltrate Brigands Motorcycle Club, he's ready to use everything he's learned to get revenge on the people who killed his family . . .